PUFFIN BOOKS

Goblin Games

Jake Lancing lives in Somerset. When not writing about adventure-seeking, football-playing angels, he spends his time avoiding work, listening to very uncool music, growing his hair, and helping the government to catch spies.* He jumped out of a plane once because it seemed like a good idea at the time.

* One of those things might not be *entirely* true.

Goblin Games

JAKE LANCING

PUFFIN

With special thanks to David J. Gatward

PUFFIN BOOKS

Published by the Penguin Group
Penguin Books Ltd, 80 Strand, London WC2R 0RL, England
Penguin Group (USA) Inc., 375 Hudson Street, New York, New York 10014, USA
Penguin Group (Canada), 90 Eglinton Avenue East, Suite 700, Toronto, Ontario, Canada M4P 2Y3
(a division of Pearson Penguin Canada Inc.)
Penguin Ireland, 25 St Stephen's Green, Dublin 2, Ireland (a division of Penguin Books Ltd)
Penguin Group (Australia), 250 Camberwell Road, Camberwell, Victoria 3124, Australia
(a division of Pearson Australia Group Pty Ltd)
Penguin Books India Pvt Ltd, 11 Community Centre, Panchsheel Park, New Delhi – 110 017, India
Penguin Group (NZ), 67 Apollo Drive, Rosedale, North Shore 0632, New Zealand
(a division of Pearson New Zealand Ltd)
Penguin Books (South Africa) (Pty) Ltd, 24 Sturdee Avenue, Rosebank,
Johannesburg 2196, South Africa

Penguin Books Ltd, Registered Offices: 80 Strand, London WC2R 0RL, England

puffinbooks.com

First published 2009
1

Text copyright © Hothouse Fiction Ltd, 2009
All rights reserved

Set in Bembo 13.5/18.75pt
Typeset by Palimpsest Book Production Limited, Grangemouth, Stirlingshire
Made and printed in England by Clays Ltd, St Ives plc

British Library Cataloguing in Publication Data
A CIP catalogue record for this book is available from the British Library

ISBN: 978-0-141-32460-9

www.greenpenguin.co.uk

Penguin Books is committed to a sustainable future
for our business, our readers and our planet.
The book in your hands is made from paper
certified by the Forest Stewardship Council.

For Gabriel

Contents

I

A Sticky Situation

'Halloween must bring out the best in you,' Alex grinned as he peered into the large food mixer sitting on the kitchen table. 'It seems your cooking's improved!'

The slimy, icky, green mess inside the bowl bubbled and burped. It looked alive and not very happy about it.

A girl in a red baseball cap looked up from the mixer. 'Well, I wish your sense of humour would improve too,' Cherry replied. 'Anyway, it's not mine. I'm just on guard. Inchy asked me to stop House trying to eat it.'

A large shadow fell over the table. It sniffed hungrily, like a dog outside a pie shop.

'Eat what? Is someone cooking?'

Alex gazed at the huge figure who'd joined them and was busy making lip-smacking sounds. 'Even you wouldn't eat this, House.'

A black-haired boy strolled over. 'Well, not without ketchup he wouldn't.'

'Thanks, Spit,' said Big House flatly. 'I'll take that as a compliment.'

'*Ta-dah!*'

Everyone turned to look at the tiny person standing in the doorway. Inchy was only a metre tall, and he was dressed from head to toe in red. Red T-shirt, red trousers, red gloves. He even had a red tail made from an old football sock filled with newspaper. A large horn had been stuck on the left side of his head.

'So? What do you think?'

Silence rolled through the room like a tumbleweed. Finally, Cherry spoke:

'Well, Inchy, as the only one here with any dress sense, I can honestly say . . .'

She paused. And continued pausing.

'It's certainly colourful,' observed Spit. 'But, um . . .'

'I think,' said Alex, jumping in, 'that what we're trying to say, Inchy, is . . . er . . . erm . . .'

'What are you meant to be?' said House bluntly.

Inchy stepped further into the room. He may have been a lot smaller than his four friends but he prided himself on being the brains of the group. Their stupidity at this moment was no real surprise, but it was a little disappointing. He made a big dramatic sweep with his arms, trying to make himself look more impressive.

'You mean the long tail and horns don't give it away?'

'Oh!' cried Spit. 'You're an angry bull – that would explain why you're bright red.'

'No, he's not a bull,' said Alex. 'He's a unicorn. Must be.'

'I thought unicorns were white?' said House.

'I think you can get red ones too,' replied Alex 'They're just rare.'

'I'm not a unicorn!' shouted Inchy.

'But you've only got one horn,' Cherry pointed out.

Inchy felt the top of his head. 'Well, the other one must've fallen off. I'm a demon, you numpties!'

'Ahh!' said House.

'Mmm!' Cherry nodded.

'Course you are!' agreed Alex.

'No you're not,' said Spit. 'You're not big enough. Besides, don't you think it's a bit inappropriate to be dressed as a demon? What with us being angels?'

'It's not inappropriate,' sniffed Inchy huffily. 'It's ironic. And anyway, size isn't everything! Besides, I'm not fully grown yet. I may be huge one day and then you'll be sorry!'

Spit smirked. 'Maybe. But speaking as one who has slain a demon,' he said smugly, 'I can assure you that they are a lot bigger than you are.'

'I think we know that, thanks, Spit,' said Cherry. 'We were all there, remember?'

The gang looked at each other, all silently casting their minds back over the adventures they'd had in the past few months. Since they'd been suspended from angel school and sent down to Earth to learn how to behave better, so much had happened.

Spit pushed his hands into his trouser pockets and frowned. 'Seems impossible that before all this started, we were winning footie tournaments back at Cloud Nine Academy, doesn't it?'

'I miss the Academy,' said House. 'I mean, Earth's an amazing place, but Heaven . . . It was out of this world. Just imagine having wings again, even small ones, and being able to fly!'

Alex sensed that his friends were on a dive to feeling rubbish. He stepped forward to face them.

'But think about what we've done since we've been here,' he said excitedly. 'Loads of cool stuff we would have had to wait *years* to do if we'd stayed at the Academy! We defeated a Level Four Fire Demon,' he continued, starting to count things off on his fingers. 'Battled zombies at the hospital . . .'

The gang shrugged miserably.

Alex raised his voice. 'Don't you get it? If it wasn't for us discovering some kind of demonic plot, who knows what could've happened here in Green Hill?'

'It's true,' said Cherry, her face breaking into a proud smile. 'We have done some fab stuff since we got booted out of the Academy. We shouldn't forget that.'

Alex looked over at his best friend. 'What do you think, House?'

House grinned. 'I think we've kicked some serious evil butt!'

'A good point, well made.' Spit nodded. 'But nobody ever believes us!' He paced up and down, his face a picture of frustration. 'We do all these things, but there's never any proof when it's all over. We never get to go home to Heaven, no matter what we do.'

Inchy looked over to Spit. 'You're right. It is really unfair.'

The gang fell silent for a moment.

'Anyway,' said Inchy, shaking his head as he walked over to the table, his tail scuffing the floor. 'How's the slime?'

'Green,' observed Alex. 'And sloppy. Not very nice at all, really.' He looked at Inchy, a question creasing his brow. 'So why exactly do we need it? Has it got something to do with you being dressed as a demon?'

'In a way,' replied Inchy, his large glasses slipping down his nose. 'You know how it's the Midnight Fair in Green Hill Woods tonight?'

The gang nodded.

'And you know how it's fancy dress, with a Halloween theme?'

The gang nodded again.

'Well, there's a prize for the best costume, and I'm planning on winning it. But to do that, I need the finishing touch for my outfit – demon slime. And as the real stuff's pretty hard to get hold of, I've made my own. Clever, eh? There's enough for you guys to have some too, if you like.'

'Um, thanks, Inch,' said Cherry. 'But I don't fancy trudging around the fair covered in something that looks that much like snot.'

'Please yourself,' replied Inchy, fishing out a brown paper bag from a pocket in his costume.

'What's that?' asked House.

'The final secret ingredient for the slime,' said Inchy.

Cherry shot Alex a nervous look. 'What do you mean by "secret"?'

Inchy grinned and wiggled his fingers over the paper bag like a magician.

'If I told you, it wouldn't be secret, now, would it!'

'Oh, well, that's a great explanation!' sighed Spit. 'And I suppose now you cackle insanely and pour it into the mixture, yes?'

'Exactly!'

'House,' said Alex, 'keep an eye out for Tabbris.'

House opened the kitchen door a crack and peered out. There was no sign of Major Tabbris,

Order of Raphael 1st Class, the retired Special Ops Guardian Angel who had been given the job of looking after the gang during their time on Earth. As well as being grumpy and short-tempered, Tabbris had an uncanny knack of turning up at the worst possible moment.

'It's all clear.'

With a flourish, Inchy ripped open the paper bag, shook the powdery contents into the slime and switched the mixer on.

For a moment, nothing happened. Everyone sighed in relief. The gang edged closer, peering into the bowl.

'What does it do?' asked Spit.

'It's supposed to make it fizz and steam.' Inchy frowned.

'Well, it does seem to be bubbling a bit now,' Alex observed as the mixture slowly started to fizz.

'In fact, it's bubbling quite a lot,' said Cherry.

The rest of the gang continued to stare into the bowl, unable to pull themselves away as the mixture began to expand, like dough rising.

'It looks like it's getting rather excited,' said Spit. 'Perhaps we should, ah, stand back a bit? You know, just in case something happens?'

'Yeah,' agreed Cherry. 'It's getting bigger.'

'So it is,' said Inchy, surprised. 'I wasn't expecting that.'

Spit raised an eyebrow.

'You weren't?'

With a loud pop, a particularly large bubble burst, scattering drops of slime out of the mixer and on to the table.

'Um, it's *still* growing,' said Alex, backing away as the mixture seethed and swelled towards the top of the bowl.

'But this is impossible!' said Inchy, his voice going high and squeaky. 'It's a completely harmless mixture, I'm sure of it!'

'The evidence seems to suggest otherwise,' Spit observed drily.

Another blob of goo flew from the bowl and landed on the floor.

'Quick, clean that up before Tabbris arrives!' said Cherry. 'Spit – we need a mop, quick!'

Spit was about to argue when a shout from House interrupted everything.

'Tabbris is coming!'

The gang exploded into action.

Spit dived across the kitchen to the cleaning cupboard and grabbed a mop. Cherry tried to cover the mixer with a tea towel. Alex made for the door, trying to think of a way to stop Tabbris coming into the kitchen. He'd just arrived when Tabbris threw it open, hitting him in the nose and almost knocking him out.

And House, stepping backwards out of the way, stood on the large blob of slime on the floor, and slipped.

He slid across the kitchen, skidding and screaming, and slammed into the table. Trying to steady himself, House threw out a hand. It hit the controls of the mixer, switching the speed from *Low* to *High* . . .

With a high-pitched whine, the mixer leapt into life. The tea towel covering it spun off like a frisbee, wrapping itself round Cherry's head like a turban, and the kitchen disappeared in a storm of goo.

It was like the room had been hit by a tornado of alien vomit. A green geyser erupted from the mixer bowl and splatted and sprayed everything in sight. Alex and Cherry tried to duck, but both just fell to the floor. Inchy leapt under the table, but somehow the slime still found him. House simply stood there, calmly accepting his fate. Only Spit somehow managed to stay almost spotless, as the green stuff covered every surface and every person in the room. He calmly reached over and switched the mixer off.

'Well, that went well, didn't it?' he sighed.

The rest of the gang slowly raised their heads to take in the sight of Tabbris standing in the doorway, dripping with slime. As they watched, another huge glob fell from the ceiling and landed on his moustache. It clung there for a few seconds, then dribbled horribly to the floor and started to smoke.

Alex had never seen someone literally shaking with fury before.

'*WHAT*,' bellowed Tabbris, 'in the name of all that is holy, is going on?!'

'It was an accident,' Alex answered, pulling himself up off the floor. 'Just an accident. It's the Midnight Fair and –'

'An accident?' snarled Tabbris, wiping his face with the sleeve of his tweed jacket. 'This is no accident. An explosion in an ammunition dump is an accident. A tank crashing into a china shop is an accident. This is a catastrophe! You lot are a five-man natural disaster!'

The gang felt the old angel's eyes burning into them.

'But they *are* just accidents,' said Cherry. 'We don't plan this stuff, really we don't.'

'That's what worries me,' Tabbris snapped. 'Just imagine the state the world would be in if you set out to cause trouble *deliberately*!'

Tabbris looked around at the kitchen, the gang and his own clothes. When he spoke again, his voice was low and frustrated. 'You are *supposed* to be learning something from being on Earth, not getting into yet more trouble! When will you start listening to me? You do want to get back to Heaven, don't you?'

13

'We're sorry,' said Spit.

'I'm sure you are,' said Tabbris. 'When you get caught. But "sorry" doesn't cut it with Head Angel Gabriel. He wants proof that you're becoming proper angels, not more excuses about why you're still getting in trouble! And you've been nothing *but* trouble since you arrived!'

Inchy opened his mouth, but Tabbris silenced him with a pointy finger. 'No excuses!'

With a sound almost as faint as spiders' webs being blown in the wind, Tabbris opened his wings. They spread out behind him, an impossibly huge cloud of ice-white feathers that seemed to surround the gang. When he spoke, his voice was as cold as an Arctic wind.

'You will not leave this room until you have ensured it is *spotlessly* clean – with a toothbrush. When it is, you will go straight to bed. You will remain confined to quarters for the rest of the weekend. There, you will try to remember what lessons you are supposed to be learning on Earth. There will be no dinner and – as an extra punishment – no salt on your porridge for breakfast tomorrow. Is that clear?'

'Yes, sir,' chorused Alex, Cherry, Inchy and House.

Without thinking, Spit put up his hand. 'But what about the Midnight Fair?'

Tabbris turned and looked at him, his eyes dark.

'I'm afraid, Respite, that you won't be going.'

Alex saw Spit bite his lip to keep quiet. Everyone knew how much Spit hated people using his full name.

'Right,' said Tabbris, his wings folding away to nothing as he turned to go. At the door he looked quizzically back at Inchy, whose football-sock tail was draping forlornly on the floor.

'A red unicorn?' he said, and left the room.

2
Break Out

Silent and dejected, the gang spent the next four hours mopping up the slime from all over the kitchen. It was getting dark by the time they were finished. Slowly they trudged up to their room.

'Yet again,' said Spit, 'old sausage fingers there puts the icing on the Cake of Disaster. We might have got away with it if it wasn't for your clumsiness.'

Before House could throw Spit through the window, Inchy jumped in.

'It wasn't really House's fault – I should've been more careful with that mixture. I don't think I got the measurements correct.'

'Mind you,' yawned Cherry, 'it would be weirder if something actually went *right* for us.'

Entering their room, the gang slumped down on their beds, groaning almost as loudly as the ancient bedsprings.

'I was really looking forward to the Midnight Fair,' said Inchy. 'I spent ages on this outfit.'

'Don't worry,' said Alex. 'I've got an idea what we can do tonight.'

'What do you mean?' said Cherry warily. 'This isn't one of your stupid plans that gets us into even more trouble, is it?'

'It's not stupid, it's brilliant – even if I do say so myself.' Alex grinned.

'What is it, then?' asked House.

'Simple,' replied Alex. 'We're going to stay here, like Tabbris said –'

'*That's* your plan?' interrupted Spit with a sneer. 'What's so great about an evening in here listening to House's Third Stomach-Rumbling Symphony?'

'Let me finish,' said Alex. 'We're going to stay behind, like Tabbris said, *and* we're going to go to the Midnight Fair!'

'He's finally lost it,' said Cherry, shaking her head sadly. 'It's the air here on Earth — it's sent him completely nuts.'

'I think she's got a point,' said Spit. 'And I never agree with anything Cherry says. I think I need to sit down.'

Cherry pulled a face at Spit, who returned the gesture.

'Anyway,' said House, 'we can't sneak out. Tabbris is bound to check in on us, isn't he? And if he sees we're not here, we'll be in even bigger trouble.'

'But we will be here.' Alex grinned, pulling something from under his bed. 'See?'

'See what?' said Cherry. 'What *is* that, exactly?'

'It's a guy!' said Alex. 'Remember? We all made them last week, ready for Bonfire Night.'

Cherry stared at the thing Alex was holding. It

looked like a scarecrow that had been run over by a combine harvester.

'But it's rubbish,' she said.

The rest of the gang nodded in agreement.

'But not if I do this,' said Alex.

With a flourish, he pulled back the scratchy blankets on his bed, put the guy in, and arranged the covers back over it.

'See?' He smiled. 'Now it's me! In bed! Asleep!'

'Can't be,' said Spit. 'It's better looking.'

'Are you serious?' asked Cherry.

Alex nodded. 'Of course I am. It's not like Tabbris comes in here and pokes us, is it? He'll never know we've gone. It's foolproof!'

'No,' said Spit, 'it's the proof of a fool. The idea's nuts. Not worth the risk.'

'I'm not sure,' said Inchy. 'When Tabbris comes to check on us, he usually just looks in through the door. The chances are he'll see precisely what he's expecting to see – the five of us in bed.'

For a few moments, the gang were quiet.

'OK,' said House. 'I say we go for it. What have

we got to lose? We're in so much trouble anyway, this isn't going to make any difference.'

'Everyone else?' asked Alex. Inchy and Cherry nodded quickly.

'Fine,' sighed Spit. 'I'm not staying behind. But don't blame me when it all goes pear-shaped.'

'Brilliant!' said Alex. 'Well, we'd better get a move on – Tabbris will expect us to all be in bed and asleep in twenty minutes. So grab your guys, guys!'

'At least mine looks like a real person,' said Inchy, tucking his guy into bed. 'I did it to scale and everything.'

Spit looked over to where House was struggling to wrestle his guy down from the top of the wardrobe. 'Remind me which one is the biggest dummy . . .' he muttered.

Finally, all five guys were in place.

'You really think Tabbris is going to be fooled by this?' asked Spit. 'He may be old, but he was in Special Operations, remember? He was an elite agent – one of the best. He's not going to be taken in by a bunch of stuffed dummies.'

Alex didn't have a chance to respond as the familiar creak of the loose step at the bottom of the stairs echoed through the house.

'Tabbris!' hissed Cherry.

'Perfect!' said Alex.

'How do you mean?' asked House.

'Well,' explained Alex quickly, 'Tabbris must be coming to look in on us now. All we have to do is hide under our beds and wait and see what happens. If he's fooled by the dummies, we're fine. If he twigs, we just jump out and say we were playing a little practical joke.'

'He's nearly here,' hissed Cherry.

'Come on!' whispered Alex.

Stealthily, the gang all disappeared under their beds.

Tabbris's footsteps fell soft and sure on the uncarpeted stairs. His walk was march-like and regular, like a heartbeat for the house. The footsteps came closer and closer until finally they stopped. For a moment, there was silence, then the bedroom door creaked open with a faint squeak, like a mouse being squeezed through a mangle.

21

Tabbris's head eased round the door, staring into the dark room. The gang held their breath, waiting for Alex's ploy to be discovered. After what seemed like a century, Tabbris pulled his head back and the door groaned shut. His footsteps retreated along the landing, down the stairs, and faded away.

Alex could hardly stifle the chuckle bubbling in his stomach as the gang emerged from under their beds.

'You're feeling smug, aren't you?' said Cherry, brushing herself down.

'Absolutely!'Alex nodded.'Tabbris has swallowed it hook, line and sinker! Great or what? Actually, no, make that *fantastic* or what?!' He rubbed his hands together. 'Now let's get into our fancy dress and get out of here!'

While the rest of the gang changed, Inchy busied himself knotting sheets together. A few minutes later, a dark rope of bedclothes was lowered from the window. The gang slipped down it, leaving the guys silent and innocent in their beds, and sped off towards Green Hill

Woods. Above them the moon hung full and quiet, an all-seeing eye on the world below.

At the end of Eccles Road, the gang turned left on to the footpath that led to the woods. Cherry led the way, threading through the night-time shadows. As well as being the only girl in the gang, Cherry had by far the most unusual fashion sense. Back at Cloud Nine Academy, she had been voted Worst Dressed Cherub for three years in a row. A fact that Spit took great delight in reminding her. As the five angels trooped along in the darkness, he saw a new opportunity.

'So, Cherry,' he said, coming up alongside her. 'You do know tonight's meant to be fancy dress, don't you?'

Cherry's eyes narrowed. 'What?'

'Well,' said Spit, 'I just wondered why you hadn't bothered to dress up, that's all. Seems a little unfair on the rest of us.'

'I *am* in fancy dress. I'm the witch from *The Lion, the Witch and the Wardrobe.*'

'Really?' replied Spit in mock surprise.

'Yes, really,' said Cherry through gritted teeth. She was very proud of her Halloween outfit, even if it hadn't been difficult to create it – her own wardrobe was pretty big.

'I see.' Spit looked Cherry up and down. She was wearing purple and green striped leggings, a black dress pulled in at the waist with a brown army belt, a yellow shirt with a huge pointy collar, and sunglasses. Bangles on her wrists jangled with every movement, while an enormous tiara made from a metal coat-hanger gleamed from her hair. 'I thought she was supposed to be beautiful and elegant.' He was pretty sure her costume was something she'd worn only last week.

Cherry ignored him. She knew hers was the best outfit in the gang. Inchy kept tripping over his tail as it swished around his feet. House was doing a good impression of Frankenstein, with ripped clothes and bolts through his neck, but the effect was ruined by the large bar of chocolate he was holding. Spit had just thrown an old bed sheet over his normal clothes to make himself look like a ghost, and Alex, for reasons known only to himself, was dressed as a pirate, right down to the eye patch and cardboard cutlass. Every now and again he kept shouting, 'Ah-hargh, me hearties!'

As it didn't look like Cherry was going to be easily provoked, Spit just sighed.

'This isn't a good idea. You do know that, don't you?'

'Who are you speaking to?' asked Inchy.

'Anyone who'll listen.'

'What do you mean it's not good?' asked House. 'It's great! We're going to the fair, Tabbris is none the wiser, and our fancy-dress outfits are fantastic!'

'But I still think Tabbris is bound to find out,' grumbled Spit. 'And the chance of a fun night out dressed like this isn't worth the trouble we'll be in when he does.'

'Look,' said Alex, flipping up his eye patch to wink at the gang. 'We're not just doing this for fun.'

'What do you mean?' asked Inchy.

'Think about it,' Alex continued. 'We're going to a Midnight Fair, on Halloween. Can you think of a better place for demons to make mischief?'

Spit stifled a sarcastic laugh. 'Do me a favour! This is just a fair. Somewhere normal people can have a bit of fun scaring each other by dressing up as things they don't really believe in. A demon wouldn't be seen dead here.'

'It's the perfect cover!' cried Alex. 'Just think about it. With everyone in Halloweeny fancy dress, no one's going to notice if something odd happens or someone – or something – weird slips by.'

'I don't believe it!' snapped Cherry, pointing at Alex with her wand (an old radio aerial with tinsel wrapped round it). 'How many times do you have to be told that we're not meant to be on Earth to look for demons? We're here to behave well and get back to Heaven. That's all we should be thinking about!'

The gang muttered agreement.

'I know that,' said Alex. 'And that's the best thing about the fair. If anyone asks, we can just say we are there for fun. So no one can blame us if we just *happen* to spot anything weird, or out of the ordinary, or really horribly evil.'

'But what if we do?' asked House nervously.

'We'll come up with a plan!'

Before anyone could object, a sudden shriek cut through the night.

'It came from over there,' said Spit, pointing ahead.

'Sounded like someone in trouble,' said House, his Guardian Angel instincts kicking in. 'Come on!'

Before anyone could stop him, House raced forward. The footpath was lit with occasional electric lights, but the way was still dark and dreary. Shadows snatched at the gang as they ran. Branches whipped at their faces and roots did their best to trip them up.

Another scream. Closer.

'This way!' yelled House, still belting ahead.

The gang burst into a small car park on the edge of Green Hill Woods. Ahead, they saw two figures. One was a woman in a pointy hat and long, flowing clothes, carrying a big patchwork bag. The other figure looked like a boy of about the same age as the gang. He was trying to wrestle the bag away from her.

'Give it to me! Give it to me!' yelled the boy.

'Get off me, you ruffian!' shouted the woman.

'Oi!' bellowed House. 'Get away from her!'

Both the woman and the boy turned in surprise at the sound of Big House's voice. For the first time, the gang got a look at the boy's face. It was green and covered with horrible crusty warts. He had a long hooked nose and greasy hair that hung down to his shoulders.

For a moment the gang stood frozen in shock. Then, shoving the woman to the ground, the boy ripped the bag from her hands and raced off into the woods.

3
Trick or Treat?

Alex raced up to the woman and helped her to her feet as House and Spit dashed over to the edge of the shadowy woods and peered into the darkness. There was no sign of the boy. He seemed to have melted into the trees as if he'd never existed.

'Looks like he got away,' said House apologetically. 'Sorry about that.'

The woman shook her head. 'Don't worry,' she said mysteriously. 'He won't get very far – the trees aren't friendly to people like him.'

'Yes, er, right,' said Alex, rather puzzled by the strange comment.

'That was quite an amazing mask he was wearing,' observed Cherry.

Inchy nodded. 'It looked almost real, didn't it?'

The woman finished brushing herself down and straightening her clothes, and turned to the gang.

'I'm Serena,' she said.

'I'm Cherry, and this is Alex, Spit, Inchy and House,' said Cherry. 'I like what you're wearing,' she added, trying not to sound too jealous. Serena's pointy hat stood tall and shimmered with silver thread. Her dress was long and the colour of autumn leaves. It seemed to be made of a thousand tiny patches of cloth all stitched together. Around her neck hung an old key, threaded on a leather thong.

'You like it? Really?'

Cherry nodded. 'It's much better than my outfit. You actually look like a witch.'

'That's because I am a witch,' said Serena.

The gang looked at each other and instinctively took a step backwards.

Serena smiled, her eyes wide. 'A *white* witch.'

'Oh, well, that makes it OK, then' said Spit sceptically.

'Yes it does, actually,' explained Inchy. 'White witches are good witches.'

'Exactly,' said Serena. 'We white witches like to feel at one with the world around us. We talk to the voices of the wind. The spirits in the trees, the animals . . .'

House looked over to Alex. 'Is she a bit cuckoo?' he muttered.

Alex tried not to laugh. 'What was in your bag?' he asked. 'I hope it wasn't anything valuable.'

Serena's face fell. 'My magical charm bracelets. I make them from things I find in the woods or on beaches. I was on my way to sell them at the Midnight Fair. My charm bracelets are very popular. They bring good luck and positive energy. People swear by them.'

'Swear that you're mental, maybe,' whispered Spit to House.

'Luckily, not all my bracelets were in the bag,' continued Serena. 'But now I'll have to go back to my shop to collect some more. Oh, well.'

'Do you want us to nip back to your shop for you?' offered Alex.

'No, that's very kind,' Serena smiled, 'but I'll be fine. It won't take me long. You get along to the fair now.'

Just then, House spotted something on the ground. Picking it up, he walked over to Serena. 'Is this one of your bracelets?'

'Why, yes, I believe it is!'

'There are more over there,' Inchy said. 'They must have fallen out of your bag when that boy ran off.'

Serena picked up the bracelets. She counted them quickly and gasped.

'What's wrong?' asked Cherry.

Serena turned and looked at them. Her face was serious, the whites of her eyes almost glowing in the moonlight.

'Five bracelets . . . For five brave friends!'

'You're going to use the word "Fate" now, aren't you?' guessed Spit. Serena looked like just the sort of person who would believe in superstitious stuff like that. She probably didn't walk under ladders and avoided black cats too.

'Fate!' said Serena in a deep voice. 'Yes, that's exactly what this is! Here. These are for you.' She reached out and handed each of the gang a bracelet.

'No, really, we can't accept them,' said Alex as Serena tied one around his wrist. 'You need them to sell.'

'You must take them,' said Serena. 'They are obviously *meant* for you. It's not for us to argue when the decision has already been made.'

Cherry looked at the last bracelet as Serena finished fastening it on her wrist. It was a thin band of tiny shells and pieces of driftwood threaded on fine wire. It sparkled and glimmered in the moonlight.

'Now,' said Serena, 'to say thank you for coming to my rescue, I will add an extra enchantment to your bracelets.' She closed her eyes and waved her hands above her head in an elaborate pattern.

'By the powers of the forest!' she chanted in a

deep voice. 'By the powers of the winds and the waves! By all the blessed power of the light, I make this spell! May these bracelets protect these kind young people! May they shield them from the darkness! And may they grant each of them their heart's desire!'

Spit shook his head. 'Totally crackers,' he hissed.

Alex poked him in the arm. 'Don't be rude!' he whispered back.

'There!' said Serena, opening her eyes.

'What? No twinkly lights?' muttered Spit. But this time Serena heard him.

'Magic isn't all about show, young man,' she said stiffly. 'Just because my spells aren't flashy, that doesn't mean they don't work. You wait and see if your wishes don't come true.'

'Wishes?' said Cherry, raising her eyebrows. 'Are you serious?'

'Of course!' Serena replied. 'Each bracelet will grant you one wish. And I wish you joy with them! Goodbye – and thank you again!'

With that, Serena practically danced off back down the road that led towards Green Hill, the darkness folding in around her like a blanket on a cold night.

'Charm bracelets!' giggled Spit. 'Magic wishes?'

'Well, I don't care if they're magical or not. I think they're rather nice,' said Cherry, spinning her bracelet on her wrist.

'Well, you would, wouldn't you? You're a girl. Girls like things like bracelets.'

'And what's wrong with that?'

'Nothing, except that it's a bit wussy and sappy. Lads don't fuss with stuff like that. It's pointless.'

'Er —' began Alex, spying the colour rising in Cherry's cheeks, but it was too late to stop the argument now.

'"Pointless"?' said Cherry in a dangerous voice. 'Are you saying that what girls think is pointless?'

'Well, maybe not pointless exactly,' Spit shrugged, 'but it's just not reliable, is it? You're too ... emotional. Yes, that's it. Girls are too emotional. That's why they like silly sparkly things — because it makes them feel nice.'

The rest of the gang backed away. They knew Cherry was about to explode.

'*Nice?*' Cherry yelled. 'You think girls are only interested in feeling nice?'

Spit opened his mouth to say something else inappropriate and unnecessary, but Cherry was too quick for him. She leapt, cat-like, across the car park and pinned him to the ground.

'Are you going to take that all back?' she demanded.

'Back where?' Spit smirked.

Alex, Inchy and House instinctively moved away. Spit was an expert at winding Cherry up, but even he pushed his luck too far sometimes. And when he did, the resulting explosion could make Bonfire Night fireworks look pretty weedy by comparison.

'Don't try to be more annoying than you already are!' snarled Cherry. 'Take back that stupid stuff you said about girls!'

'No, I won't, because it's true,' said Spit. 'Girls just aren't as good as boys!'

Cherry's eyes bulged furiously.

'I wish you knew what it was like to be the only girl in this gang,' she yelled. 'Then you'd understand!'

Before Spit could even open his mouth to reply, a cold wind seemed to rush into the car park from all directions at once. Then, with a blinding flash, the world exploded with blue light.

4

Be Careful What You Wish For

'What on Earth was that?' asked Alex, as the blast
of light faded.

The rest of the gang rubbed their eyes, half-
blinded.

'It came from Cherry's bracelet,' Inchy remarked.
'She was on top of Spit, saying something about
being the only girl in the team, then there was a
flash . . .'

House looked around.

'Well, we're all OK. Maybe it was lightning or something. I mean –'

Spit screamed.

The sound was so loud that it seemed to tear the air.

The gang turned to see Spit leap up off the ground and point down at Cherry, shock and terror etched into his face.

'It's me! I'm down there! What's going on? How can I be standing here and be down there as well? I don't understand!'

Alex was at Spit's side in an instant. He gripped his shoulders and stared into his eyes.

'Mate! What's wrong? Everything's OK! You're fine. We're all fine!'

Spit looked back at him with eyes filled with fear.

'It's not OK! Everything's wrong! I'm down there – look! LOOK!'

Again Spit pointed at Cherry, his finger shaking. Alex looked.

'That's Cherry,' he said. 'She's OK too.'

'No she's not,' said Cherry.

Alex, House and Inchy turned. Cherry was getting to her feet, but she looked very uncomfortable. It was like she was learning to stand or walk for the first time. She stumbled a little and pulled at her dress like it didn't feel right.

'Cherry?' said Alex. 'Are you OK? You're acting a little strange.'

Behind him, Spit had stopped screaming and now sat sobbing into his hands. This was very odd. Spit never cried. Never. He prided himself on it, and said crying was for girls.

Cherry looked from Alex to Spit, then back to Alex again.

'I'm not Cherry, I'm Spit,' she said.

Alex was confused. 'I'm sorry, what?'

'What's Cherry on about?' asked House, confusion written in deep lines across his face. 'Why's she talking like Spit?'

Alex's face dropped so fast gravity took a while to catch up.

'Oh no . . .'

Inchy caught on at the same time.

'But it's not possible . . .'

House didn't know what anyone was talking about, so just kept quiet.

'Well,' said Spit from Cherry's body, 'it seems it is possible. Apparently Serena the witch is actually a witch, and her magic bracelets do actually work.'

'They grant wishes,' sighed Alex, hardly believing the words he could hear himself saying. 'Which means . . .'

'Exactly,' huffed Spit. 'Cherry wished that I knew what it was like to be the only girl in the gang. Well, now I do, don't I? I'm in her body and she's in mine.'

Cherry pulled her new Spit-face from her hands.

'But I don't want to be a boy,' she said. 'I don't want to be Spit. I want to be Cherry again, in my own body. It's mine and I want it back!'

House looked at Spit. 'And now Spit's talking like Cherry! This is nuts!'

'They've swapped,' said Inchy. 'Spit's now in Cherry's body, and Cherry's now in Spit's. Got it?'

House couldn't even shake his head.

'Thanks for the scientific observation,' said Spit, pulling the witch's tiara off his new head.

'Hey! Be careful with that!' yelled Cherry, jumping up from the ground in her own new body. 'It took me ages to make.'

'Look, don't start arguing again,' sighed Alex, stepping between them. 'That's what got us into this mess.'

'Really?' Cherry retorted. 'Well, if it wasn't for your stupid plan to sneak out to the fair we wouldn't have been here *in the first place*, would we?'

'Look, you can hardly blame me for all this!' protested Alex. 'It's not like I knew we'd run into a real witch, or that she'd give us real magical bracelets, or that we'd then have real wishes that would come true! Well, is it?'

For a moment, no one spoke.

'So what now?' asked Spit, still trying to stand up straight in Cherry's body and not doing very well.

'Why don't we just take the bracelets off?' suggested House.

The gang stared at him, all of them slightly

annoyed that they hadn't thought of that simple solution themselves.

'Good point, House,' said Alex, and reached for his bracelet. 'That might undo the magic.'

'This doesn't make sense,' said Inchy. 'Mine's shrunk. It's really tight. It won't come off!'

'Mine too!' said Spit.

'And mine!' said Cherry.

Alex, tugging at his bracelet, looked at House doing the same.

'Why don't we just break them, then? Mine's only a bit of thread with some shells and pebbles on it.'

Alex grabbed his bracelet and pulled, expecting the delicate strands to snap easily.

Nothing happened. It was like trying to bend an iron bar. For a few moments the whole gang pulled and strained. House and Alex even tried breaking each other's bracelets, without success.

'It's no good,' groaned Inchy, his fingers straining against the bracelet. 'They're too strong!'

'But it's impossible.' Alex grimaced. 'How can they be so tough?'

'Must be the magic,' said Inchy. 'Magical objects are often stronger than they appear.'

Eventually, they all gave up.

'This is ridiculous,' said Cherry.

'Do you mean what's happening to us, or the style of this dress?' asked Spit, yanking at the unfamiliar garment he was now wearing.

'Don't stretch it!' squawked Cherry.

'Enough of the arguing!' yelled Alex in frustration.

Silence reigned briefly.

Alex took a deep breath. 'We need to work out a way out of this.'

'I've got an idea,' said Cherry.

'Yeah, well, if it's as good as this costume –' started Spit, but a scowl from House cut him short.

Alex turned to Cherry. 'Well?'

'We might be able to use the wishes to undo this,' Cherry suggested. 'Serena said that each bracelet would grant one wish. Now, I used up the one on *my* bracelet when I was in my own body. But I'm in Spit's body now – so why don't

I just use the wish in *his* bracelet to get everything back the way it was?'

'I don't think that's a very good idea,' said Inchy. 'I mean, that first wish didn't seem to work very well, did it?'

'What are you talking about?' grumbled Spit. 'Seems to have worked all *too* well as far as I'm concerned.'

'Except that Cherry didn't actually wish for the two of you to swap bodies, did she?' replied Inchy. 'She just wished that you knew what it was like to be a girl. She didn't say anything about her wanting to be a boy, but that's what happened. I think maybe these wishes are a bit, you know, unpredictable.'

'Oh, great!' spluttered Spit. 'So we've got a bunch of bracelets with crazy wishes in, is that what you're saying?'

'I'm just saying that it's probably not a good idea to try undoing a wish using another wish, OK?'

'Hmph,' snorted Spit.

'Don't make my nose make that horrible sound,' said Cherry. 'It's revolting.'

Alex walked to the centre of the group, drawing

everyone's attention. He looked at each of them in turn. 'I have a plan,' he declared, grinning.

'Oh no . . .' groaned Spit. He looked down at his new dress in disgust, as if things couldn't get any worse.

'No, really!' Alex protested. 'This is a good one. Let's go and find Serena. Maybe she'll know how to undo the magic – she made it after all. But until we find her, we need to be really careful that no one wishes for anything else, got it?'

Everyone nodded warily.

'Good,' said Alex. 'Now we know that Serena was heading back into town. She can't have got far. Let's get after her. Follow me!'

5
Which Witch?

'There!'

Everyone looked to where House was pointing. The gang had been hurrying towards Green Hill for ten minutes and were just coming to the outskirts of the town. A few hundred metres ahead was a tall figure striding speedily away from them.

'It's Serena!' said House. 'Come on!'

The gang picked up their pace.

'Let's run,' suggested Cherry, obviously keen to get out of Spit's body and back into her own.

'I don't think that's a good idea,' replied Spit. 'I haven't quite got the hang of how your legs work yet.'

Walking as fast as they could, the angels slowly closed the gap. By now, there was a steady stream of people coming the other way, heading out of town towards the Midnight Fair. The streets were filled with people who looked like they'd just been hit by an exploding dressing-up box. Vampires, ghosts, ghouls, werewolves and pretty much anything else from the darker side of fairy tales, milled along the pavements. It wasn't hard to keep Serena in sight – her huge pointy hat made her easy to spot – but she had long legs and it was harder to catch up with her in a crowd.

The gang were almost in shouting-distance when she suddenly turned a sharp corner and disappeared from view.

'Come on, we can't lose her!' said Alex, urging the gang into a jog. They ran around the corner, expecting to see Serena just ahead of them, and stopped dead.

The scene before them was like something

out of a comedy horror film. Green Hill High Street was a sea of people.

And every single one of them was dressed as a witch.

There were witches on corners waiting for buses, witches buying kebabs from vans, witches strolling along, arm in arm, singing 'Old MacWitchy Had a Farm' at the tops of their voices. There were young witches, old witches, tall witches and short witches. It was, thought Alex, *witchtastic*.

'Where'd she go?' said House, staring blankly at the mass of witches. 'Which one is our witch?'

'Is that her?' suggested Cherry, pointing. 'That one – next to the one with the long black cloak.'

'They're all wearing long black cloaks!' retorted Spit.

'How about her?' said Inchy.

'Do you mean the one who keeps tripping over her pumpkin?' asked Alex. 'Or the one holding a mop instead of a broomstick?'

'There!' cried Cherry triumphantly. 'Going into that tent!'

Sure enough, Serena's distinctive hat was just disappearing into a large marquee that had been erected in the town square. Instantly, the gang raced after her, zipping in and out of crowds, jumping over the occasional bubbling cauldron, and avoiding rather too many black cats, until they skidded to a halt at the entrance to the tent.

'Why do you wear these stupid high heels?' Spit asked Cherry, trying not to lose his balance. 'They're rubbish for running.'

'Well, I wasn't expecting to be racing around Green Hill tonight, was I?' Cherry replied. 'Anyway, you can't talk – what's with these really tight trousers? Are you afraid your legs are gonna fall off or something?'

'They're not tight, they're cool,' said Spit. 'Something you obviously don't understand.'

'Can we save the fashion arguments for later, girls?' Alex barked. 'It's time to find that witch!'

With that, he charged into the tent. The rest of the gang quickly followed.

'Well, that's not something you see every day, is it?' commented Spit.

The tent was large and packed wall to wall with yet more witches.

Only these ones were dancing.

'Grab your partners, do-si-do!' yelled a fat witch standing on a platform at the far end of the tent. She was holding a microphone and standing in front of a band dressed as skeletons. She seemed to be thoroughly enjoying herself, slapping her thigh in time with the music.

'It's a barn dance,' said Inchy. 'Someone shouts out what to do and everyone does it. I think.'

'But they all look so stupid,' said Cherry, as a witch and a zombie spun past.

'Ah, more people to join in!' shouted a rather tipsy man dressed as a wizard. 'May I have this dance, miss?'

Without waiting for a reply, he grabbed Spit, who suddenly found himself being whisked down through the crowds with everyone clapping.

'Alex!' he yelled. 'Help me! He thinks I'm a girl!'

'Well, you can't blame him, can you?' spluttered

51

Alex, helpless with laughter. 'You are wearing a dress!'

The rest of the gang collapsed in hysterics as Spit was spun around the tent by the wizard, who was obviously very excited to be dancing with a pretty girl.

'You're a lovely dancer, young lady!' He beamed.

'I'm *not* a lady!' shouted Spit, stamping down hard on the wizard's toes. The man yelped in agony and let go of Spit long enough for him to push the wizard away and run, or at least hobble, back to the gang.

'See, there is a use for high heels after all!' Cherry grinned.

'If you say so,' snapped Spit, giving her a hard look. 'Anyway, where's House?'

Alex looked around. House was nowhere to be seen. Then Cherry pointed.

'There he is. But what's he doing?'

Big House was tiptoeing along the wall of the tent towards a small group of witches who were chatting in a corner. One of the witches was wearing a pointy hat that looked a bit like Serena's. Even from this distance, though, the gang could see that it wasn't her.

Unfortunately, it looked like House couldn't.

'Quick!' cried Alex. 'Stop him!'

But it was too late. With a completely un-announced pounce, House leapt clean through a pair of werewolves and seized the unfortunate pointy-hatted witch.

'Gotcha!' he yelled, hauling her off her feet and into the air. 'Alex! Everyone! Look! I've got her!'

Unsurprisingly, the witch started to scream. Then her friends joined in. The combined effect sounded like a bag of cats being trampled by an elephant. They tried to pull their friend away from House, but the big angel was having none of it.

'I'm not letting go! I'm not! You change Spit and Cherry back, you hear? Or I'll . . . I'll . . .'

Alex arrived just in time to stop whatever it was that House was about to do.

'House! It's not her!'

The other witches rounded on Alex as the rest of the gang appeared.

'Do you know this young scallywag?'

Alex nodded at the witch who'd spoken. She was thin and knobbly, like a really large Twiglet. Except that she was wearing a black dress covered in sequins and carrying a plastic cauldron.

'Then perhaps you can explain why he is attacking Brenda?'

Brenda gave a squeal, which dislodged her pointy hat, revealing a set of features completely different from Serena's.

'I'm on the town council, young man!' snapped one of the witches, whacking House on the bottom with her broom. 'And unless you put my friend down *this minute*, I'll have no choice but to have a stiff word with your parents!'

Blushing the same colour as Cherry's hair, House carefully set Brenda the witch back on her feet, while trying to rub his stinging bottom at the same time. She turned round, scowled and adjusted her black wig.

'Really sorry,' House mumbled. 'I thought you were someone else.'

Before the witches could start shouting again,

Alex dragged House off into the crowd, the gang following behind.

'I thought it was Serena and I didn't want her to get away!' House explained.

Alex smiled. 'Well, if it *had* been her, she wouldn't have got away, that's for sure! Now, let's calmly have another look around. She can't have gone far.'

Slowly, the gang spread out through the tent. Apart from the barn dancers the place was packed with people bobbing for apples and buying indoor fireworks. It was so busy that it was hard to stay together, and the five angels drifted apart, each keeping a lookout for Serena as best they could.

Which in one case was not very well at all.

'This is ridiculous.' muttered Inchy to himself. All he could see in front of him was a forest of legs and bums. It was all well and good for the others, but he was just too small to be of any use in a crowd. 'I wish I was tall enough to see over people's heads,' he said.

Instantly, wind whipped up under the sides of the tent, threatening to send it soaring into the sky. The bracelet on Inchy's right wrist flared like a camera flash. Several people turned round to see who was taking a picture.

Blushing furiously, Inchy stared down at his bracelet. The light had faded, but that didn't make him feel any better. How could he make such a stupid mistake? He felt sick, his stomach twisting into knots as he waited for something to happen. But nothing did. He didn't seem to be any taller, and it seemed that none of the gang had noticed the flash. Was the bracelet faulty somehow? Was that possible?

As Inchy stood thinking, he felt himself suddenly pulled into the air. For a moment he panicked, thinking that his wish must somehow be coming true. Then a familiar voice boomed in his ear.

'You'll see better up here,' said House, plonking Inchy down on his shoulders. 'Found anything?'

Dizzy with relief, and how high he now was above the floor, Inchy tried to push all thoughts of his wish out of his mind. Luckily, it didn't seem to have worked this time – he'd be more careful from now on. In front of him and all around was a mountain range of witches' hats and pointy false noses. Inchy narrowed his eyes and concentrated.

He grabbed House's ears.

'Don't make any sudden movements, but isn't that her just going out of the door?'

House looked. Inchy was right – Serena was just slipping out of a side-door in the tent. Waving to Alex, Cherry and Spit, Inchy directed them to the door. A moment later, the gang were outside.

'Over there,' hissed Inchy. 'She's gone into that shop. The one called Moondust.'

'Then let's follow her. And quietly,' said Alex.

House edged forward and slowly pushed the shop door. It slipped smoothly and silently open, like the yawning mouth of some huge monster. Alex led the way into the gloom, closing the door behind them.

Inside, the shop was like nothing any of them had ever seen before. The air smelled dusty and sickly sweet. Despite the noisy street party going on nearby, it was silent, as though all sound had been sucked out of it. The shop was crammed with shelves, boxes, crates and counters, all stacked on top of each other in a haphazard and very dangerous-looking way. It was like walking through a cupboard that was half-frozen in a state of collapse. Alex felt that at any moment, the whole place was going to come crashing down around them.

Heading deeper into the shop, Alex was amazed at what he saw. From the rafters hung feather-decorated dreamcatchers and crystals on thin silvery chains. Wind chimes and bells dangled dumbly in the window. Mirrors winked from beams and a row of unlit candles stood like sentries along a wide window sill. There were so many shelves of crystal balls, boxes of incense, bottles of strange liquid and odd things made out of wood, that it was impossible to work out where the walls finished and the floor, or indeed the ceiling, began. Alex couldn't quite believe a shop could be filled with so much rubbish – or that anyone would ever want to buy it.

'Spooky, isn't it?' murmured a voice.

Alex turned. He could just about make out Inchy and the rest of the gang among all the junk the shop was stuffed with.

'I guess,' he whispered back. 'But it's just a shop. Serena must've slipped out the back.'

'But don't you think it feels weird too?' continued Inchy with a shiver. 'Like something's watching us?'

'What do you mean?'

Inchy never had a chance to answer, though, as, with a yell that shattered the darkness, a shadowy shape leapt straight at the gang.

6
Moondust and Magic

As a trainee Guardian Angel, Big House knew exactly what to do in this sort of situation: a simple manoeuvre that would immobilize the attacker without hurting them. Back at Cloud Nine Academy, he'd read all about it, practised it, even done it under exam conditions.

Unfortunately, the gang weren't in the Academy at that moment. So instead of carrying out a silent but superbly executed counter-measure, House sprang at the figure, screaming very loudly that whoever or whatever they were, they were going to wish they hadn't been born. Unfortunately, he misjudged his leap and flew *past* the figure, arms flailing, hands flapping and legs kicking.

'No, House!' yelled Alex, but it was too late. He tried to grab his friend, but all he managed to clasp was thin air.

House continued to fly *through* the air until eventually he met the floor. Or would have done, if it hadn't been for all the shelves in the way.

En route, his left arm caught in a string of fairy lights hanging from the ceiling. As he pulled them down with him, they snagged a rack of velvet shirts, tugging them after. House's right arm achieved a similar effect by grabbing at the curtain to the changing room. It came away very easily and with little complaint, bringing down a large chunk of the ceiling to join in the fun.

Entangled in the fairy lights and curtain, House staggered into a large bookcase standing against one wall. With a groan, it toppled over, slamming into the bookcase behind it, which toppled over in turn. The effect House had achieved was quite remarkable. Shelves and bookcases all around the room tipped over and fell, like a giant set of dominoes, throwing strange packets and objects in all directions.

Alex, lost in shock at the sheer scale of the destruction House had created, didn't notice the crystal ball as it spun through the air. It made a sound like a large gong as it thwacked him on the head. He crashed to the ground, stars spinning in front of him and a ringing sound bouncing around his skull.

From his new vantage point, he was able to watch the rest of the gang diving for cover. Cherry narrowly avoided three didgeridoos that tried to spear her to a wall. Inchy disappeared into a basket filled with odd bits of material. Spit managed to crawl behind a large, worn blanket box. And the shadowy figure that had so scared them vanished under an avalanche of incense sticks, candles and bags of beads.

Dust settled. Silence stood for a while, then slowly slipped from the room.

'Alex?'

'Spit?'

'That you, Cherry?'

'Anyone seen Inchy?'

A bespectacled head appeared from the material basket, like a cobra for a snake charmer.

'Here,' said Inchy. 'What about House?'

'I'm OK!' came a muffled call from somewhere underneath a large pile of everything the shop sold.

'House?' called Alex.

The mound shook, like a mountain disturbed by a minor earthquake. Then it exploded to reveal House.

'Hello.'

'Wondered where you'd got to.' Alex smiled.

'Me too,' said House. 'What happened to that other person?'

The gang looked left and right and it was Cherry who spotted their assailant, flat out on the floor at the back of the shop, pinned down by a very ugly wooden statue of a cat-headed Egyptian god with weight problems.

Pulling themselves free of the debris, the gang stumbled and crawled towards the figure.

'But what if he's dangerous?' asked Inchy.

'Well, he did attack us with a badly painted stick,' said Spit drily, cutting House off by prodding him in the belly with it.

'I think it's *meant* to be a magic wand,' Cherry said doubtfully.

'Well, whatever it is,' said Alex, 'who was carrying it?'

Spit leaned over to check, but was immediately forced to leap backwards as the person stood up, scattering beads in all directions.

'Serena!' said the gang all at once.

'Yes!' yelled Serena. She pulled herself to her full height and contorted her face to make it look as scary as possible. Unfortunately, it just made her look constipated.

'That's me – I'm a witch and I'm armed!'

She snatched the wand back from Spit and

waved it threateningly, like a drunken conductor.

'So listen up and listen up good! I want you all to go – no! – to *vanish* from this place! Yes that's it! Vanish!'

She waved her wand. Her tattered clothes quivered in the air like the shreds of a burst balloon.

'And if you don't go voluntarily, then I'll have no choice but to er . . . erm . . . oh yes! Smite you with my mighty magic!' Serena cried, following up her threat with a very unconvincing attempt at an evil laugh.

The gang watched her inquisitively to see what was coming next. Spit sighed and examined his new colourful nails.

Serena finally stopped and peered down at them.

'Oh, it's you! The ones from the wood. You helped me when that nasty boy stole my bag of charm bracelets!'

'Yes, that's us,' said Alex. 'And it's those bracelets we want to talk to you about. You see –'

Alex didn't get a chance to finish as Serena, with a heavy sob, thumped back down on to the shop floor.

'You've come to complain, haven't you?' she whimpered. 'You don't like them because they don't work!'

'No,' said Alex. 'It's not that at all!'

'It is,' wailed Serena, tears now falling. 'I did my best with that spell, I really did, but I'm just not very good at them. Some witch I am. No wonder people call me Silly Serena. I'm about as magical as a packet of crisps.'

'Well, they're pretty magical,' said House. 'Particularly if it's late at night and there's something really good on TV.'

'House!' said Alex warningly.

'Sorry,' muttered House. 'Just getting hungry, that's all.'

Alex turned back to Serena.

'Look, about that spell, Serena. It worked.'

Serena looked up, sniffing and wiping her nose. 'I beg your pardon?'

'Your spell worked,' said Alex. 'The bracelets

grant wishes, just like you said they would. Cherry made a wish and it made her and Spit switch bodies. And now we don't know what to do about it.'

'But that's impossible!' said Serena, folding her arms and leaning back against the shop counter. 'I'm rubbish at this magic stuff! None of my spells have ever actually *worked*.'

'Well, this one didn't exactly go according to plan,' said Cherry. 'The wish I made went a bit wonky. But it did work. I know you think you're looking at a boy when you look at me, but you're not. I'm actually Cherry. A girl. I am most definitely NOT a boy.'

'I don't believe you,' replied Serena, shaking her head. 'It can't be true. You're having me on! This is some sort of Halloween joke.'

'I wish it was,' said Alex. 'But it's not.'

'Prove it!'

The gang fell silent.

Alex spoke first.

'How about one of us makes a wish? That would do it.'

'You have to be joking!' exploded Spit. 'Look what happened last time! No way!'

'For once I agree with Spit,' said Cherry. 'The first wish didn't work out well, did it? The last thing we need is another one going wrong and causing us even more hassle.'

'Well, let's just make it a safe wish,' said Alex.

'I don't think we should,' said Inchy, feeling his throat tighten at the thought of his own close escape. 'We don't know how these wishes work.'

But Alex's eyes had already lit up.

'Don't you dare!' shouted Spit, trying to put a hand over Alex's mouth. He was too late, though.

'I wish this room was tidy again!'

'No!' screamed Spit as the bracelet on Alex's wrist flared with power.

'What have you done?' groaned Inchy.

'We'll soon find out,' said Cherry. 'But as it was Alex's plan, it's probably not going to turn out well.'

As Cherry spoke, strange currents were already starting to whizz through the air. The winds picked up, getting faster and faster, until it was almost as if there was a tornado in the room. The gang grabbed hold of the only secure thing they could find – the shop counter – as the wind began to pick up objects from the floor and whirl them around. Faster and faster the tornado spun, until it seemed like every object in the whole shop was whirring around above the gang's heads, missing them by millimetres.

Suddenly, and without warning, the storm ceased. The roaring tornado simply vanished as if it had never been.

The room was empty. Every single item that had been on display had disappeared along with the howling winds.

'Well,' said Spit finally, standing up. 'Empty is one definition of tidy, I suppose.'

The others looked nervously over at Serena. How would she react to losing a whole shopful of merchandise?

For a long moment, she simply stayed sitting on the floor, staring into space. Then she leapt to her feet as if she'd been stung.

'That was *amazing*! I've never seen anything like

it! Proper magic! Did you see it? Did you? And all because of my spell! That's amazing! I *am* a witch! Wait till I tell the rest of the coven about this!'

'So you believe us, then?' said Alex. 'That the bracelets work?'

'Believe you? Of course!' Serena beamed. 'I can't doubt the evidence of my own eyes! I don't see what good it's going to do you, though,' she continued. 'I've no idea why or how that spell worked. I just made it up on the spot. It must be a fluke. But what an amazing fluke! If I can just remember the spell and use it again on the rest of the bracelets, I'll make a fortune!'

'Um, I hate to point this out,' said Cherry nervously, brushing Spit's dark fringe out of her eyes, 'but didn't all your bracelets just vanish with all the other stuff?'

'What?' replied Serena. 'Oh no. I don't keep them in here – they're in the other room at the back, with all the magical books.'

'Even so,' continued Cherrry, 'don't you think the bracelets are too dangerous to just hand out to the public? I mean –'

Cherry wasn't given time to finish. The front door to the shop smashed open.

'It's that kid again!' cried Serena. 'The one who stole my bag! And he's brought his friends!'

It was true. Standing in the doorway were five figures. They were small and slender, and as well as their warty green goblin masks, they were wearing rather nifty knee-length camel-coloured coats. Their shoes were particularly shiny and their hair slicked back and surprisingly neat. Their fingers were weighted down with huge gold sovereign rings.

The figures stepped forward into the shop, polishing their rings on their coats in a distinctly unsettling manner.

It was Inchy who noticed first.

'Um, Alex?'

'What is it, Inch?'

'You know those horrible masks they're wearing?'

Alex nodded.

'Well,' said Inchy. 'I don't think they're masks after all.'

71

7
The Key of Aziel

'Goblins!' yelled Inchy.

Alex looked confused. 'Pardon?'

'They're goblins!' Inchy shouted again. 'Real ones! They're not wearing masks at all!'

'Aren't goblins supposed to be, well, primitive? You know, rabbit-skin pants and stuff?'

Spit nodded. 'These look more like dodgy second-hand car dealers.'

'And what's with the coats?' asked Cherry. 'Bad taste or what?'

'If they're goblins, then I'm a hobbit,' said House.

'Then I'd say you're a hobbit, mate, ain't ya?' said the lead goblin in an ugly, snarly voice. He walked up to House, looked him up and down, and prodded him with a bony green finger. 'Allow me to introduce myself. I'm Narl and these are my four . . . associates.'

The other four goblins nodded.

'Now,' said Narl, 'can we do this all politely? Or do my mates here have to get a little bit . . . clumsy?'

'What do you want?' asked Alex.

'A word with the witch,' replied Narl simply.

'You've already taken her bracelets,' said Cherry hotly. 'Why don't you just leave her alone?'

'She's got something she shouldn't have. Something that belongs to somebody else. Just let us have it and we'll be off.'

'We can't do that,' said Alex.

Narl shook his head slowly and deliberately. 'Wrong answer.'

Without another word, the goblins leapt forward. Taken by surprise, the gang fell back as the green-skinned intruders made for Serena.

'Oi! Leave her alone!' cried House, rugby-tackling Narl, and bringing the goblin to the ground.

'Nice move,' said Inchy, impressed.

'Watch out, Inch!' screamed Alex as a goblin flew through the air towards him.

Inchy ducked, but too late. The goblin slammed into him, sending them both sprawling.

Within seconds, Alex, Cherry and Spit were grappling with a goblin each too. House was wrestling with Narl on the floor. Although the goblin was much smaller and skinnier than House, he wriggled like a fish, and was almost impossible to pin down. Finally, though, House managed to grab both Narl's arms and press them against the floor.

'OK, OK, I surrender,' said the goblin, his body going limp.

'Really?' said House, relaxing. 'Oh good.'

Narl grinned. 'Only joking, matey!'

And with that, Narl brought his bony knee up into House's stomach, knocking the wind out of him. Leaping to his feet, Narl turned and bounced across the shop, grabbing the key chain round Serena's neck.

SNAP!

'I've got it!' crowed Narl. 'Fun's over, boys!'

He sprinted out of the shop and disappeared into the night. Before the gang had time to react, the other goblins bolted for the door too. One of them paused in the doorway and winked.

'Bye now! Nice doin' business with ya!'

With that, they were gone.

'Check on Serena,' shouted Alex to House, as he helped Spit to his feet.

House ran over to Serena, who was sniffling and wiping her nose.

'Are you OK?'

Serena nodded. 'But he took it – he took my necklace.'

'What happened?' asked Alex, as the rest of the gang came over.

'The goblins nicked her key necklace,' said House. 'Maybe that was what Narl was after back in the car park. He didn't get it then, so he went off to collect reinforcements. It must be pretty important to them. They've gone to a lot of trouble to get it.'

Alex turned to Inchy.

'You're the brainy one, Inch. What can you tell us about goblins?'

Inchy screwed up his face as he struggled to remember. He'd once read a whole book about mythical creatures, but it seemed like a long time since he'd been sat in the library at Cloud Nine.

'They're nomads,' he said finally. 'Travellers and wheeler-dealers. From what I remember, they roam around the world with a magical market, setting it up in one place, then disappearing the next day. It's called the Goblin Market.'

'How imaginative,' muttered Spit.

Ignoring Spit, Inchy continued, 'The market is supposed to be really weird, but it's not evil. Goblins aren't like demons or anything like that – they might trick you into paying too much for something, but I've never heard anything about them doing anything really nasty.'

'What, like mugging people and stealing their

belongings?' said Cherry. 'Doesn't seem very nice to me.'

Inchy shook his head. 'You're right. It's odd. Not usual behaviour.'

Alex folded his arms. 'Well, I'm guessing it's no coincidence that these goblins have turned up in Green Hill at exactly the same time as the Midnight Fair. What we need to do now is work out what's going on.'

'And why's that?' asked Spit. 'I mean, why do we have to get involved? Can't we just go home and forget all about it?'

Alex ignored him and looked at Serena, who had now stopped sniffing.

'That Narl character said that you had something that didn't belong to you and that they wanted it back. What's the story with the key, Serena? What's so special about it?'

Serena shrugged sheepishly. 'A few weeks ago, a lady came into the shop looking for a magical object called the Key of Aziel. I didn't have it, but I said I would ask some of my friends in the magical community. I didn't expect them to find it, but to my surprise one of them knew where the key was and agreed to send it to me. But when it arrived, it looked so beautiful and sparkly that I couldn't part with it. It felt like Fate had meant for me to have it. So I decided to keep it for myself. I told the lady that I couldn't find it, and refunded her money.'

'But if she found out that you did have the key after all,' said Alex, 'then she might feel that it didn't really belong to you and try to take it. What was this woman called?'

'She said her name was Mrs Shepherd,' replied Serena.

'Did you notice anything odd about this Mrs Shepherd?' asked Spit. 'Did she look a bit shifty? Evil perhaps? Like the sort of person who would mix with goblins?'

Serena looked at Spit strangely. 'Not at all. She seemed very nice.'

'The Key of Aziel,' mused Cherry. 'I haven't heard of it. Inchy?'

Inchy shook his head. He looked disappointed. He never liked to admit there was something he didn't know, but he was finding it hard to concentrate. The collar of his T-shirt felt tight – as if it was two sizes too small. And his shoes felt tight too. It was almost as if he was growing.

Inchy gulped. His wish! Back in the tent of witches he'd wished that he was taller, so that he could see over people's heads. He'd thought that nothing had happened then, but could it be that the wish was coming true after all?

Nervously, he looked around at the rest of the gang. Had any of them noticed what was happening to him? He hoped not. After the disaster of Cherry's wish, the last thing he wanted to do was admit that he'd made a wish too, especially after they'd all agreed not to.

'What about you, Serena? Do you know anything about this key?' asked Alex.

'Well, I did find something about it in one of my books,' replied Serena. 'It's in the back room. Hold on a minute . . .'

The gang waited as Serena disappeared into a cluttered storeroom at the back of the shop. She returned a moment later with a huge leather-bound book. She quickly thumbed through the pages, until she found the right one.

'There!' she said, turning the book round so that the gang could see.

'That doesn't sound good,' said Cherry darkly.

'What do you mean?' asked Alex, fearing the worst.

Cherry read from the book: '"This is the Key of Aziel. Beware all who hear of it. Despair those who find it. Magic surrounds it. Chaos will rule. Portals will open."'

'Portals?' asked House. 'What does that mean?'

'Portals are like doors,' explained Inchy. 'Doors between different dimensions.'

'Exactly,' said Cherry, scanning the page again. 'And it says here that the Key of Aziel has the power to open *all* portals. It can open those to Heaven and also . . . the Other Side.'

'Oh no, not that again,' groaned Spit.

8
Growing Pains

'Oh, great,' said Inchy, slumping down on the floor. The sound of tearing cloth echoed around the room.

'What was that? Did you just rip your trousers?' giggled Cherry.

'Um, I must've caught them on a splinter or something,' replied Inchy hastily. He glanced down. His trousers had certainly split, but he suspected that might have less to do with a splinter than the fact that they were now too small for him. 'Anyway, there are more important things to worry about than my trousers. Portals to the Demon Dimension and stuff like that? It's no coincidence that this is all happening on Halloween.'

'What do you mean?' asked Serena, looking confused.

'Well,' sighed Inchy, glad that no one seemed to have noticed his unexpected growth spurt. 'Halloween's one of those weird times when strange stuff happens.'

Inchy gulped. It was a little difficult to talk, as his collar now felt like it was trying to strangle him. 'Halloween isn't just about dressing up and pumpkin lanterns and trick-or-treating,' he continued. 'It's the time when the boundary between Earth and the Other Side is supposed to be at its weakest.'

'Mumbo jumbo,' said Spit.

'It's not mumbo jumbo,' retorted Serena indignantly. 'It's perfectly true.'

'And those goblins didn't seem very mumbo jumbo,' replied House. 'They were pretty real if you ask me.'

Inchy frowned. 'And now we've discovered that someone is hunting for the Key of Aziel, which is supposed to be able to open a portal between Earth and the Other Side. It doesn't take much imagination to work out who's behind it.'

'Oh, great,' muttered Cherry. 'More demons.'

The gang were quiet for a few moments. With the possible exception of Alex, none of them wanted to get tangled up with demons again – it nearly always lead to trouble, and definitely always to a horrible punishment from Tabbris. But from what Inchy was saying, it sounded like they might not have much choice.

'Let me just get this straight,' said Spit. 'You're saying that Halloween is the best night of the year to open a portal and that all someone needs to do that is use the Key of Aziel?'

'That's about right.' Inchy grimaced.

'Then we need to get it back,' said House.

'And fast,' said Inchy. 'Whoever has the key is going to use it tonight.'

As Inchy spoke, something really surprising happened. His T-shirt ripped at the seams and fell to the floor.

'Oh,' said Inchy.

The gang and Serena stared.

'I, um, think it shrunk,' said Inchy, trying to laugh it off. 'You know, in the wash.'

'I think it's the other way round, isn't it, Inchy?' said Spit, looking closely at his friend.

Inchy didn't know what to say.

'Stand up for us, would you, Inch?' asked Spit and for once he actually sounded concerned.

Slowly, Inchy raised himself to his feet.

'Wow!' said House.

'You've grown!' said Alex. 'You're as big as me! That's not possible!'

'It's the bracelet,' admitted Inchy. 'I made a wish by accident. I wished that I was taller. I think I've been growing ever since.'

Spit frowned. 'We weren't supposed to be making any more wishes.'

'Yeah,' agreed Cherry. 'It could be really dangerous.'

'I know,' said Inchy. 'I didn't mean to do it. It just slipped out.'

'Do you feel OK?' asked Alex with concern.

Inchy shrugged. 'Fine. I quite like it, actually. It's not easy being the small one all the time. This wish might be a good thing.'

'I doubt it,' said Spit. 'Serena, you said that before tonight none of your spells had ever worked.'

'That's right.'

'Well, I reckon that the reason the spell you cast on the bracelets tonight *did* work was because you were carrying the Key of Aziel at the time.' Spit sighed. 'Think about what it says in the book – "Despair those who find it. Magic surrounds it. Chaos will rule".'

'What are you saying?' Cherry asked.

'Well,' said Spit, 'it sounds to me like the key can do magic, but it creates chaos at the same time. That's why the wishes have come true in an odd way. You wished that I knew what it was like to be a girl, and your wish came true – but not in the way you meant it. Alex wished for the shop to be tidy again, and the shop was made tidy – all the stuff in it vanished. That wasn't what you meant to happen, was it?'

Alex shook his head.

'So what I'm trying to say is that the bracelets are even more dangerous than we thought. The chaos magic twists the wishes so that they will never come true in the way we want them to.'

Inchy gulped. 'So what does that mean about my wish?'

'I don't know,' admitted Spit. 'But I think that we should try to reverse it as soon as we can. To do that, though, we're going to need to get the key back.'

Silence fell over the room. Cherry looked across at Alex. 'Isn't this the moment where you turn to us all and smugly say, "I have a plan"?'

'Yes,' said Alex. 'But I haven't got one.'

The gang were stunned.

'Really, I haven't,' said Alex.

'Well,' said Cherry, 'why don't we start by going to the Midnight Fair. If the goblins *are* running it, then Narl and his pals will have gone back there. And they're the ones who have got the key.'

'Makes sense to me,' agreed Alex.

'But what about me?' asked Serena. 'If it wasn't for me giving you those bracelets, you wouldn't be in this mess. How can I help?'

Inchy looked at Serena.

'Have you got any more books like this one in that storeroom?'

Serena nodded. 'I have a whole library back there.'

'Then we need you to stay here and look through every one of them for any mention of the Key of Aziel. You might be able to find out something about how to reverse our wishes.'

'Right,' agreed Serena.

'OK, team,' said Alex. 'Let's go to the fair . . .'

Even Spit was impressed by the Midnight Fair. As the gang walked into Green Hill Woods, they found a narrow, winding path lit by carved pumpkin lanterns. These were hung from plaited ropes which were strung from tree to tree. They seemed to float in the air, strange ghoulish faces laughing silently in the night, dripping yellow light into the woods. As the gang burrowed deeper into the trees, the sounds of laughter and excitement grew and grew until the air was alive with an orchestra of noises, voices and music.

Finally, the gang arrived at an arched gateway over the path. It was woven from willow branches threaded with coloured silks, exotic feathers and twisted vines. Hanging from the top of the arch was an enormous piece of wood carved into a sign that said: *The Midnight Fair.*

Beyond the entrance, it looked as if the fair was well underway, with crowds of people in fancy dress milling around in swirls of bright colour, and making a joyful noise. Mouthwatering smells reached their noses. More pumpkin lanterns provided a warm glow, as did countless flaming torches.

'I think we should stick together,' said Alex. 'We don't know what this fair is like or what to expect. Anything could happen.'

'Safety in numbers.' Inchy nodded.

'Sorry,' said Spit, looking up at Inchy, who was now even taller than he was. 'I didn't quite catch that – your voice seems to be a little bit . . . *high*.'

Inchy winced at the bad joke, but the rest of the gang could see he was secretly pleased with his new-found height. They couldn't help but laugh.

'You know, if you keep getting bigger, you could *grow* on me.' Cherry smiled.

'That's a *tall* order,' said Big House. 'I think you're *stretching* the point.'

'Be fair, you two,' said Alex. 'Inchy can't help it. I think that making fun of him is the *height* of bad taste!'

'Come on, guys,' groaned Inchy. 'Enough with the jokes. Let's start looking for that key.'

Trying their best to not snigger, the five angels slipped through the willow arch and entered the Midnight Fair.

It was like stepping into another world. Their jokes about Inchy's height were forgotten in an instant as the sights and smells of the market dazzled them. Everywhere they looked, the gang saw something they wanted to check out. To their left was a stall selling sweets unlike any they'd ever seen, each with a tremendous name like, 'Choco-hate!' and 'Cavity Cave-in!' or 'Suck it and Flee!' Next to that, another stall-holder was beckoning customers into a canvas cavern filled with weird and wonderful foods: everything from jars of pickled moon-cheese and pots of exotic spices, to huge barrels of elderberry wine and baskets of sweet-scented fruit bread. The shelves were heaving and groaning with things none of them could even describe. The gang stood, stunned, overcome with an urge to look at and taste and touch everything.

'Can we start over there?' asked House, pointing.

Everyone turned. A few metres away stood a stall selling rolls crammed with roast pork, stuffing and crackling. A whole pig was slowly turning on a spit over a pile of glowing embers, fat dripping and spitting in the heat. The smell drifting across to the gang was a whole new world of delicious.

'I think all this growing's made me hungry,' said Inchy. 'So I say yes!'

The rest of the gang followed him over to the counter.

'Here you go, my dears!' said the stall-holder, handing House a huge roll filled with roast pork. 'The best-tasting, free-range, fully organic roast-pork roll you'll ever taste!'

'How much,' gabbled House, reaching into his pocket for some money.

'On the house!' chuckled the stall-holder.

'What? Free?' said House, surprised.

'Absolutely free!' cried the stall-holder, passing out more pork rolls. 'One for each of you. Just you enjoy them – that's the only payment I'm interested in!'

With a shrug, House took a bite. His teeth sank into the soft bread, crunched through the crackling, slipped through some stuffing and cut into the succulent pork. His eyes rolled back in his head. His mouth seemed alive with taste, bursting with the sensation of utter deliciousness.

'Nice?' asked Alex.

All House could do was nod as he swallowed and took another huge bite, his eyes closed in ecstasy. A few seconds later, the whole gang were munching their way through their own enormous roast-pork rolls and moaning in delight. His one finished, House turned back to ask if there was any chance of seconds with extra crackling.

The stall-holder laughed. 'Certainly, young sir.'

'Thanks!' said House, taking the roll and looking at the stall-holder properly for the first time. Then he gulped nervously and backed away.

'Alex?'

'Mmm?' replied Alex, his mouth still full of pork.

'Is it me, or is the stall-holder a *you-know-what*?'

Alex looked up. House was right. The person running the stall was small and wiry, and although he was wearing a white apron rather than a brown coat, the face that looked out from under a flat cloth cap was undoubtedly bright green. On top of that, it was the ugliest face Alex had ever seen. In fact, it looked like it had been hit repeatedly with a mallet.

'Um, yeah. That's a goblin,' said Inchy.

House nodded. 'Thought so.'

'Shall we, er, move along?' suggested Spit quietly.

'Let's do that,' said Cherry.

Slipping into the crowd, the gang beat a hasty retreat from the hog-roast stall. A moment later, they found themselves standing at a smaller stall selling drinks.

'Lemonade? Orangeade? Cherryade? Pumpkin-ade?' sang the stall-holder. Who was also small, thin and decidedly green.

'It's another one!' breathed House nervously.

Alex looked from stall to stall. There was no escaping the fact that every single stall at the market was being run by goblins.

9
The Goblin Market

'Well, I think we can safely say that the Midnight Fair and the Goblin Market are one and the same thing,' said Inchy.

'But you said the Goblin Market is safe, right?' asked Alex.

'That's what the books say,' replied Inchy.

Alex took a deep breath. 'OK, well, maybe Narl and his mates are renegades or something. This place doesn't seem too bad so far.'

It was true. None of the many human visitors

seemed the slightest bit worried. Presumably because they thought that the stall-holders were in fancy dress just like everyone else. Alex had to admit that it was quite a clever idea – the goblins were way too ugly to have ever been able to blend in among humans, but by making the Midnight Fair fancy dress, they had got the humans to blend in among the goblins instead, without even realizing it.

'Young sirs and lady!'

As if by magic, a particularly skinny goblin had appeared right in front of them. He was clutching what looked like a very large coconut. Spit scowled as the goblin blew him a kiss.

'I'm *not* a lady!' he muttered.

'Yes?' said Alex to the goblin. 'What do you want?'

'You look like a footie fan to me,' replied the goblin.

'Um, yeah, I am,' agreed Alex.

'And I'd bet my front teeth you're an expert at keepy-uppy,' grinned the goblin, revealing that any front teeth he had once owned had disappeared.

'I suppose.'

The goblin pointed at a large board nailed to a nearby tree. On it were written lots of odd names and next to each name, a number. The top name was Muckstinker. The number next it was 379.

'That's the scoreboard,' said the goblin, throwing the coconut to Alex. To his surprise, he realized that it was actually a football that looked like it had been made out of the hair from a yak. 'The rules are simple. Beat thirty, you win a goldfish. Beat sixty, you win a bag of toffee. Beat a hundred, you get the star prize!'

'Star prize?' said Spit sceptically.

The goblin proudly held up a box. On the top, inscribed in gold lettering, were the words: *Dragon Egg*.

'Rare as a dishonest goblin,' said the goblin with a toothless smile.

'What if I beat three hundred and seventy-nine?'

'That record has stood since 1966.' The goblin grinned. 'And in all that time, no one's ever got close.'

Alex flicked the ball into the air with his right foot. 'Until now.'

For a few minutes, the gang watched as Alex, with next to no effort, kept the ball in the air, flipping it from foot to foot. They were very soon bored. And Alex had only reached 46.

'Look,' puffed Alex, sensing the gang's boredom, 'I might be a while. Why don't you lot go and look around while I finish off here?'

'What happened to sticking together?' objected Cherry.

'Inchy says it's safe,' replied Alex without taking his eye off the ball. 'And he's never wrong.'

'But what about our mission? We're supposed to be stopping someone from opening a portal to the Other Side!'

Alex's face was a mask of concentration. 'This won't take long. We'll find the key once I've broken that record. I'll catch you up.'

'Fine,' snorted Cherry. 'Come on, guys.'

The gang wandered on through the fair. From every stall and stand, sights and sounds tugged at them, begging them to stroll over and investigate.

'Hey there, handsome! You look like a strong guy,' crooned a female goblin as the gang passed by.

House looked confused. 'Are you talking to me?'

'I sure am. Come over here!'

At the nearby stall, the goblin presented House with a huge sledgehammer, so big she couldn't lift it, only drag it along the ground to him. Next to the stall sat a wooden box with a battered metal stump sticking up from it. At the back of the box, a pole stretched four metres up into the air. On top of it was an enormous brass bell.

'Time to test your strength,' said the goblin loudly. 'Smack that lump of metal there with the hammer. Hit it hard enough to ring the bell and you win a prize!'

The goblin turned to the crowd.

'Anyone here think this honest-looking young fella has a chance?'

The crowd cheered as the goblin handed House the hammer.

'Well?' said the goblin.

House shrugged. It didn't seem too difficult. After all – hitting things was one of his best talents. With a mighty swing, he brought the hammer up in a swift arc and slammed it down. A metal ringer rattled up the pole, but it didn't reach the bell. In fact, it barely made it halfway.

'Not bad,' said the goblin. 'Try again.'

This time, House swung with all his strength. He did better, but he was still miles from the bell.

'Never mind,' said the goblin comfortingly. 'What about your big friend?'

'Who?' replied House.

'I think he means Inchy,' said Spit. 'Have you looked at him recently?'

House turned and found himself looking directly into Inchy's face. His eyes bulged. 'You're as big as me! Bigger!'

Inchy looked down – the ground did seem to be getting further away by the minute.

'Well?' said the goblin.

'I'll give it a go,' sighed Inchy. Taking the hammer from House, he swung it over his head without even looking and thumped it down.

Shooting a trail of sparks, the metal ringer shot up the pole and crashed into the bell, which went spinning off into the darkness with a loud clang. The crowd gasped.

'Amazing!' breathed Cherry.

House just stood there, speechless.

'But . . .' was all Inchy could say.

'Incredible!' screamed the goblin. 'Unbelievable! I bet you could lift me clean over your head, couldn't you?'

'Try it!' yelled someone from the crowd.

'Yeah, go on!' cried someone else.

Without any apparent effort at all, Inchy lifted the goblin off her feet and over his head. The crowd went wild.

'Do me!'

'And me too!'

Inchy grinned. 'One at a time! I'll catch up with you guys!' he shouted as more people came over to see what had happened.

'Not you as well,' sighed Cherry. 'Don't you want to get your wish undone?'

'Not yet!' replied Inchy. 'It's fun being the strong one for once. Just give me five more minutes.'

'Fine,' growled Cherry. 'But no more than that.'

'Let's go that way,' House pointed. 'It looks a bit quieter.'

They found themselves taking a right turn down a narrow row of stalls. This part of the market seemed darker than the rest, but the mouthwatering smells intensified.

'They're all selling food!' whispered House.

At each stall, they found themselves swept up in a heady world of taste and wonder. Plates and bowls and cups of free samples were thrust at them by enthusiastic goblins, all desperate for them to try their wares. They sampled cheeses fermented in caves two miles underground and others so mouldy they were more fur than cheese. They drank herbal drinks that sparkled and fizzed and zinged. And so it went on for stall after stall, until the only thing in their minds was food and drink.

But it was one particular stall that finally

caught House's attention. It was empty, apart from a single object in the centre of the counter. It was the largest pie House had ever seen. The pastry was a stunning golden colour and patterned with leaf shapes and berries.

'A whole metre wide,' said the goblin stall-holder proudly. 'Stuffed with duck, rabbit, venison, pork, chicken, beef, pigeon and partridge! I call it the King of Pies.'

'The King of Pies,' repeated House. 'How much?'

'*How* can you still be hungry?' demanded Cherry. 'We've had enough free food already to last a week!'

'I tell you what,' said the goblin. 'How about a little challenge. If you can eat the whole thing, you can have it for free. Fail, and it'll cost you twenty pounds.'

'Done!' said House instantly. 'Got a knife and fork?'

Seconds later, House was demolishing the humungous pie. His arms were a blur as he shovelled the delicious pastry into his mouth.

'I think we could be here for some time,' sighed Spit.

Cherry nodded.

'I think I'll take a stroll,' said Spit. 'See what else is going on.'

'I'm coming with you,' replied Cherry quickly.

'Why?' asked Spit. 'What's wrong?'

'Nothing's wrong,' said Cherry. 'I'm just not going to let you wander off unaccompanied while you're in my body, that's all. I dread to think what could happen to it.'

'I'd be very careful,' said Spit, pretending to be hurt.

'Whatever,' said Cherry. 'Come on.'

They had only taken a few steps, though, when Cherry stopped.

'By the way,' she said. 'Didn't we come to the fair to *do* something?'

Spit frowned. 'Like what?'

'I can't remember. But it's like we've all forgotten something, or been distracted . . .'

As Cherry spoke, her eyes scanned the throng of people still enjoying the Midnight Fair. Just then, from the corner of her eye, she spotted a goblin staring back at them from the crowd. His face seemed tantalizingly familiar, but she couldn't work out why.

'Do you recognize that goblin?' she asked.

Spit looked. 'He seems familiar,' he said. 'And he looks very smug.'

Cherry summoned all her powers of concentration. Where had they seen that goblin before? Suddenly, and without warning, a name popped into her head: Narl.

And then the penny dropped.

'We've got to get back to the others NOW!' said Cherry. 'Quick!'

'What? Why?' protested Spit.

'No time to explain. Come on!' Cherry raced back to the pie stand and literally dragged a protesting House away from the last quarter of the King of Pies, back to the Test Your Strength stall, where Inchy was completely surrounded by goblins, all asking him to lift them above his head.

'Put them down, Inchy!' screeched Cherry. 'We have to get back to Alex.'

'I'm here,' said Alex, appearing beside her. 'And guess who's the new keepy-uppy champion of the Midnight Fair?'

'Forget that,' snapped Cherry. 'It's all a diversion.'

'What?'

'All these games and tricks, they're designed to get us to forget why we came here – to find the Key of Aziel. I'd forgotten too until I saw Narl. You remember – the goblin who stole it from Serena. The football and the strength competition and House's pie, it's all a diversion. The goblins are trying to stop us from finding the key!'

The rest of the gang looked dumbstruck.

'She's right,' said Inchy. 'I'd completely forgotten. There must be some sort of magic in the air.'

Alex felt like a fool.

'Right,' he said. 'We have to get out of here quick.'

'Oh, it's too late for that,' said a scratchy voice. It was the stall-holder from the hog-roast, but now his voice was far less friendly. 'I think it's time for you lot to have a little talk with the boss.'

105

The gang looked around. They were surrounded on all sides by goblins.

'This way,' said the lead goblin.

Before they could protest, the gang found themselves being barged and pushed towards a large striped tent on the edge of the fair. They tried to fight back, but the scrum of goblins was too strong. In a moment, they were bundled inside.

The inside of the tent was dark, but the gang could see that it was crammed with goblins. There was no way out.

'What now?' whispered Spit.

For a moment, there was silence. The goblins stared at the young angels, their eyes glowing redly in the dim light. Then, just ahead of the gang, the crowd parted to reveal a tall, fat figure sitting in a large and expensive-looking leather chair, carried on the shoulders of four goblins. On the figure's head was a small trilby hat, and he was dressed in a smart, dark blue pinstripe suit. Like all the other goblins, the figure's face was green and warty, but with the addition of a horrible scar that ran diagonally across his features.

And as the scarred goblin caught sight of the gang, he bared his sharp teeth in a terrible snarl. 'What are *you* doing here?'

10
Double-Crossed

'Well?' bellowed the goblin again. 'Why are you here?'

The gang stared, unable to think of anything to say.

The hog-roast goblin bowed low. 'They are looking for the key, Your Majesty.'

'Looking for the key?' boomed the Goblin King. 'What about our agreement, our contract?'

'What's he on about?' muttered House.

'Dunno,' Cherry hissed back. 'But whatever it is, he seems pretty cross about it.'

The Goblin King shook his head angrily. 'Why would she ask *us* to find the key and then use humans to look for it too? What is it she's not telling me?'

'Just a minute,' said Alex, plucking up all his courage and stepping forward to look at the Goblin King. 'Have you found the key?'

The king's expression of outrage abruptly changed to sheepishness.

'Um, well, no. Not exactly. But we will! We're goblins! We can find anything! But it takes time. Your mistress must have patience.' The goblin's voice had gone from threatening to wheedling in one big jump.

Alex turned round to the gang, who were looking thoroughly confused.

'I reckon the goblins are working for this Mrs Shepherd and he thinks we are too,' he whispered. 'And Narl hasn't got back here yet with the key.'

'So what?' House whispered back.

'So maybe we've got a few minutes to find out more about what's going on.'

Alex turned back to the king.

'Our mistress is most displeased with your lack of progress! In fact, she's furious.'

The Goblin King looked shocked. So shocked that he forgot to speak, giving Alex the chance to steam ahead.

'Tell me at once what you have discovered so far, and we might be able to persuade her not to cut off your earlobes and eat them for supper!'

The king's face crumpled into a picture of misery.

'We've got search parties out everywhere! Not a stone, or tree, or cow in this town will be left unturned, I swear it.'

'They're searching under cows?' repeated Spit. 'That's what I call being thorough.'

'Very well,' said Alex grandly. 'When you find the key –'

Before Alex could finish, a familiar figure burst into the tent, rushed up to the king and kneeled down before him. It was the goblin called Narl.

Held in his outstretched hands was the Key of Aziel.

'Your Majesty, I bring you the key we have been searching for.'

'Pants,' muttered Alex. 'Now we could be in trouble.'

'Excellent, Narl.' The Goblin King beamed. He turned back to the gang. 'See? I told you we would find it. Go and tell Mrs Shepherd that –'

'Your Majesty, wait!' interrupted Narl, spotting the gang for the first time. 'These people don't work for Mrs Shepherd. They are in league with the human woman who had the key.'

'What?' roared the king.

'They stopped me getting the key when I caught the woman in the car park,' said Narl. 'Then when we went to the shop, they were there again, and they tried to fight us off. Why are they here? What do they want? And when can we eat them?'

'Eat us?' squealed Cherry to Inchy. 'I thought you said they weren't evil?'

Narl simply smiled a hungry grin, showing

off an alarming number of needle-like teeth.

'So,' growled the king. 'You don't work for Mrs Shepherd. Then what do *you* want with the key?'

The gang looked at each other and Inchy stepped forward. He was now almost three metres tall and the king looked a little nervous as he approached.

'Look, er, Your Majesty,' he said, 'it's true that we don't work for Mrs Shepherd. And we want the key because if it falls into the wrong hands it could be very dangerous. If you've got any sense you'll give it to us.'

'Why, what can it do?' asked the king craftily.

'It could open a door to let demons on to Earth,' said Inchy quietly.

'Demons!' chuckled the king. 'That's a good one!'

'I say we eat them,' said Narl.

'It's true!' said Inchy desperately. 'And we should know!'

'Oh, really?' said King. 'And how come you know so much about it? Are you demons too?'

'No,' snapped Inchy. 'We're not demons. We're angels!'

The king looked stunned for a moment. Then he roared with laughter.

'Angels? Not on your nelly!'

'I'm telling the truth,' said Inchy.

'Angels, he says,' snorted the king, looking up at the enormous Inchy. 'You look more like an ogre!'

The king guffawed at his own joke, and the rest of the goblins in the tent joined in, hooting obediently with raucous laughter.

'What are we going to do?' asked Cherry. 'They're never going to believe we're angels.'

'Why should they?' said Spit. 'It's not like we can do anything angel-like, is it? Not since Gabriel sent us here and stripped us of all our angel powers.'

'But there must be some way to prove it,' said Alex. 'There *must* be!'

'I wish I had my wings,' muttered House.

There was a blinding flash.

'Oops.'

'House, what have you done, you numpty?' said Alex.

The Goblin King gasped.

'Wings!' he said, pointing a wavering finger. 'You've got . . . wings!'

The gang looked at House in amazement. Jutting from his back were two huge and very beautiful snow-white wings.

'My wings!' murmured House in awe. 'My wings are back!'

'So you *were* telling the truth,' said the king. 'Interesting.'

'Yeah!' said House, flexing his muscles. 'So just you watch out!'

Without any further warning, he took three steps backwards and, with a huge thrust of his legs, he spread his wings and catapulted himself into the air.

For a moment he hung there, grinning. Then he dropped to the ground like a stone, landing flat on his face.

The gang rushed to his side. 'What happened, mate?' asked Alex. 'What's wrong?'

'I . . . I can't remember how to fly!' said House in horror, pulling himself to his feet.

'But you're an angel!' said Spit. 'Flying is what we do!'

'It must be the chaos magic,' said Inchy. 'Remember how none of the wishes come true in the way you expect? The wish must have given House his wings back, but made him forget how to fly.'

'Oh, marvellous,' said House grumpily.

Just then, another goblin rushed into the tent. 'It's Mrs Shepherd!'

'Oh no!' cried the king in a panicked voice. 'If she finds a bunch of angels here, she'll think we've double-crossed her. You have to hide. Goblins!'

Once again, the gang found themselves surrounded by goblins and shuffled off into the darkest corner of the tent, out of sight of the entrance.

'What about Inchy?' asked Cherry. 'He's too big to hide!'

'I'll crouch,' suggested Inchy. 'No, I know, I'll lie on the ground.'

'There isn't room,' said Spit. 'We can barely move ourselves.'

'She's coming!' screamed a goblin. 'She's here!'

Alex looked at Inchy.

'There's only one thing for it,' he said, crouching down to the ground and picking up a big handful of mud.

'What's that for?' said Inchy.

'The king said he thought you were an ogre, so let's make you look like one!'

With that, Alex jumped up and slapped the mud all over Inchy's face.

'Brilliant!' said Alex as Inchy spluttered. 'Just perfect! Now pull a face and try to look stupid.'

Before Inchy could object, the door-flaps of the tent were tugged open and a woman with white hair and a lined, wrinkled face entered. She shuffled on unsteady feet and leaned heavily on an old wooden cane. She wore a tweed skirt, sensible shoes and an old navy blue cardigan that looked as if a plague of moths had been dining on it for weeks. Altogether, she looked about ninety.

'*That's* Mrs Shepherd?' House hissed. 'That's the one they're all so afraid of?'

As if to answer his question, all the goblins fell to the floor, grovelling in the mud. The gang followed suit. Soon the Goblin King was the only person in the tent not on his knees. He walked forward, holding out the key in his hand.

'Here is the Key of Aziel. We have fulfilled our side of the bargain. Now it's your turn. Return our beloved Varena!' cried the king. 'Give me back my daughter!'

Mrs Shepherd laughed, and it sounded like glass shattering.

'I think not,' she said. 'I like you goblins better when you do as you're told. And while I have the princess, you will do as I command. You make pretty dreadful servants, but you do have your uses.'

The king looked as if he was about to explode.

'Give me Varena! We had a deal!'

'No, maggot,' sneered Mrs Shepherd. 'I will not.'

'Then I will not give you the key!' the king bellowed.

'Oh, really?' said Mrs Shepherd. 'Then I will take it.'

Red light exploded into the tent. Mrs Shepherd threw back her head and screamed. Her whole body seemed to quiver. Her skin darkened to a deep blood red, and her body seemed to twist and expand. Her fingernails lengthened into dark talons, black horns forced their way out of her head, and from her back erupted a pair of enormous bat-like wings.

The Goblin King fell over backwards as he tried to get away, dropping the Key of Aziel as he did so. With a triumphant snarl, Mrs Shepherd snatched up the key from the mud and raised it high.

'At last!' she screeched. 'I have the key! And now the world shall tremble!'

With a roar, a huge jet of flame leapt up around her, reaching up to singe the roof of the tent. A second later it was gone, and so was Mrs Shepherd, leaving nothing behind but a patch of scorched earth.

'Great,' said Spit. 'Another Fire Demon. Just brilliant.'

House looked at Alex. 'We're in big, big trouble.'

11
Switching Sides

'Now what?' Inchy asked no one in particular.

'Well, first we need to find out exactly what's going on here,' said Alex. 'And then we'll go from there.'

'And where exactly will we be going?' asked Cherry.

'Oh, into danger most foul probably,' said Spit. 'Scared?'

'No,' bristled Cherry. 'Why?'

'Just wondering,' replied Spit. 'As you're in my

body at the moment, I'm worried that you might wet my pants.'

Before Cherry and Spit could get into yet another argument, Alex stood and made his way over to the king, who was sitting on the ground, his head in his hands.

'Er, Your Majesty?' The king raised his head. 'Who's Varena?'

The king's eyes seemed to sink even further into his face, like they were trying to escape out of the back.

'She's my only daughter,' he said, his voice breaking. 'Shepherd kidnapped her. She's holding her prisoner in the caves further into the wood. Shepherd promised that if we found the key for her, she would give Varena back. But now she is lost! Lost!' Fat tears rolled down the Goblin King's scarred face. Suddenly he didn't seem so scary any more.

Inchy approached, towering over everyone in the tent.

'The thing is, Your Majesty,' he said, 'demons never keep their word. Ever. And now Shepherd has the key, the only way we can stop her bringing hundreds more demons to Earth is to work together.'

'So what do you suggest?' asked the king.

'Oh, you know, nothing much,' said Alex, smiling. 'A heroic rescue of the damsel in distress, some danger, and perhaps a bit of demon-smiting. Nothing too strenuous!'

The king leaned forward, his eyes suddenly steely.

'And why should I trust you? You could just be muck-born folks out to cause us goblins even more trouble!'

Alex looked serious. 'You don't have any choice. We're on the same side now. We need to stop the demon and you want your daughter back,' he said. 'It's as simple as that.'

The king stumbled to his feet and back to his throne. For a few moments he sat silently, his eyes closed. Then he stood up.

'I don't like it, but you're right,' he said. 'I could use your help. If you are angels, then you will have the best chance against Shepherd.

Narl will show you the way to the caves.'

'*What*?' said Alex and Narl at the same time.

Cherry looked the goblin up and down.

'Can we trust him?' she asked.

'It's like he said.' Narl grinned, nodding at Alex. 'You don't have any choice, do you?'

Alex looked at the gang. He knew they needed Narl to show them how to get to the caves. He also knew that he trusted the goblin about as far as he could comfortably spit a badger. But they were stuck between a rock and a hard place. Or in this case, a goblin and a demon.

'You lead the way, then,' said Alex. 'But I'll be watching you.'

'He's not the only one,' added Spit. 'I'm not a big fan of people who've suggested I'd make a good starter for lunch.'

Narl saluted the king and turned away from the rest of the goblin crowd to lead the gang out into the night. It was Cherry who spotted their first problem.

'Er, Alex?'

'Yeah?'

'What about Inchy?'

'What about him?'

'Look at him,' said Cherry. 'He's still growing. He must be four metres tall now. And the market out there is full of humans.'

'So?'

Cherry sighed. 'How do humans usually react when they see an actual giant suddenly walking around? What happens in films?'

Alex thought for a few moments, but House answered for him.

'They run around screaming their heads off?'

'Exactly,' said Cherry.

Narl looked back at the gang. 'What are we waiting for?'

'We've got a bit of a giant problem on our hands,' said Cherry. 'Inch, could you come here a minute?'

Inchy walked over. He was probably nearer four-and-a-half metres tall. Alex could have sworn he felt the ground shake slightly with each of his steps.

'Yes?'

'We need to get him out of here without the humans seeing him,' said Alex.

'Fine, we'll go out the back,' replied Narl. 'This way.'

Cautiously, House lifted up the side of the tent and peered out. There was no one in sight.

'All clear!'

On hands and knees, Narl and the gang wriggled out under the canvas. Not used to his newly restored wings, House got tangled up in the guy ropes, and Inchy's huge body nearly brought the tent down, but finally they were out in the fresh air. Behind them, the Midnight Fair was still going strong, but the Goblin King's tent shielded them from the eyes of the human visitors.

'So, Narl,' said Alex, eying the goblin suspiciously, 'where to now?'

Narl simply pointed into the thick darkness of the woods. A path, thin and grey, led off away from them, eventually fading from view in the gloom.

'How far?'

'A couple of miles,' replied Narl. 'It won't take us long to get there.'

'Well, after you,' said Alex.

Without a word, Narl headed off and the gang followed, single file, with Inchy bringing up the rear, as he kept having to duck under branches.

The path was long and made no sense at all. It wound back on itself in great loops. It zigged and zagged and zagged and zigged. And no matter how hard any of them looked ahead, the end was never in sight. It was as though someone was keeping their destination hidden in the custard-thick darkness, always moving it away from them.

'I spy with my little eye . . .' said Spit. 'Absolutely nothing at all.'

'So you can't see the caves, then?' said Narl, pointing ahead.

The gang stared.

'I don't see anything,' muttered House.

'Let's get a bit closer,' Cherry suggested.

Moving silently, the gang crept down the path. For several moments they were faced with nothing but darkness. Then, finally, they could just make out the entrance to a cavern about a hundred metres ahead.

'You've got sharp eyes,' said Alex suspiciously.

'And a sharp mind too,' retorted Narl.

A frown creased Alex's forehead. 'But when were you going to mention the cave was guarded?'

Narl looked confused.

'What do you mean guarded?' he said.

Alex just pointed.

'Oh, good,' whispered Spit hoarsely. 'Trolls.'

'And I thought demons were ugly,' said House.

A pair of trolls were standing sentry at either side of the cave entrance. The monsters were as tall as Inchy, grey-skinned and wore muscle the way most people would wear a comfortable jumper. Their thick arms looked as if their only purpose was to rip things into teeny-tiny bits and then stuff the bits into their huge, tooth-filled mouths. Their faces were thin, their eyes sharp, and their noses flat. Their only clothing was a loincloth each, and clasped in their hands they each held a fork that looked big enough to skewer a buffalo.

'Looks like someone doesn't want visitors,' said Cherry.

'Well, who are we to argue?' replied Spit.

'We can't turn back now,' said House, rustling his wings. 'We have to get that key away from Shepherd before she opens the portal.'

'And so that we can undo these wishes,' added Inchy from somewhere several metres above their heads.

'But how can we get past those trolls?' mused Alex.

'I feel sorry for them,' said Cherry. 'Look at them – all ugly and alone. It can't be much fun.'

Alex noticed the glint in Cherry's eye.

'What are you thinking?' he asked.

'Oh, nothing really,' said Cherry. 'Just that maybe I could help them out?'

Alex grinned. 'You're a genius! Hold on a minute . . .'

Reaching inside the big black bag he was carrying as part of his pirate costume, Alex produced a much smaller bag with the words *Lucky Dip* sewn on to the front. The Lucky Dip was Alex's treasure trove of weird and wonderful objects. It had never failed to contain something that would get the gang either into or out of trouble. This time, though, Alex knew exactly what he wanted. He stuck his hand into the Lucky Dip and pulled out a large bow and quiver of arrows.

Narl looked confused. 'How did that fit inside there?' he asked. The bag seemed much too small to have held the bow.

'Never mind that,' said Alex, handing the bow and arrows to Cherry. 'It's time to put your archery skills to work – you are a Cherub, after all.'

'You're not thinking what I think you're thinking, are you?' asked Spit. 'Because if you are, then I think you should know that there's a time and a place for using Arrows of Love, and this isn't it.'

Cherry strung an arrow to the bow.

'Don't do it,' said Spit. 'You don't even know if it will work. I mean, is there any chapter in the Cherub handbook about trolls?'

Cherry raised the bow, drew back the string, and took aim. The gang fell silent. They were all well aware that Cherry's marksmanship wasn't her strong point. Alex and the others held their breath.

The arrow sprang from the bow, zipping through the air.

It missed the trolls by at least a metre and smashed into a rock above them, dislodging a shower of large stones that thumped down on to their heads. The trolls didn't look very happy about it at all. They rubbed their heads and growled. Then their searching eyes found the gang. One troll raised its huge, hairy hand and pointed straight at them. The other one smiled, licked its lips and rubbed its tummy.

'But I was dead on!' said Cherry. 'There's no way I should've missed that! It's cos I'm in your stupid body! It's ruined my aim!'

'Yeah, blame someone else, why don't you?' yelled Spit. 'It's not my fault if you can't hit a barn door from ten paces! You —'

With an ear-splitting roar, the trolls charged.

12
Rescue Mission

Raising their huge forks like lances, the trolls thundered towards the gang. There was nowhere to run and nowhere to hide. The angels and Narl stood paralysed with fear.

'Quick, give me the bow!' snapped Spit.

'No way!' protested Cherry. 'You'll break it.'

'Look,' cried Spit. 'You said you missed because you're in my body. Well, I'm in yours, so why don't I give it a try?'

Before Cherry could reply, he snatched the

bow from her hands and fitted two arrows to the string. The trolls were closing on them fast.

'Two arrows?' squawked Cherry. 'Who do you think you are, Robin Hood?'

Spit ignored her. 'Right,' he muttered, taking aim. 'Let's see if your body's all it's cracked up to be.'

With a musical *twang*, Spit released the bow string. Two arrows hummed through the air, each one curving elegantly towards its target. Two arrows thunked into the two trolls. Perfect shots.

Cherry looked at Spit, completely stunned.

'No idea what your problem is,' sniffed Spit. 'Must all be in the mind.'

'Look!' called Inchy, pointing at the trolls. The huge creatures had stopped charging and instead were sitting down on the forest floor, hugging each other. Every now and again the slightly bigger one would let out a sort of groan-roar that was loud enough to rattle the trees, and stroke the slightly smaller one's bald, scabby head.

'I think that means "I love you" in troll,' commented Alex.

'Ugh. I think so too,' agreed House as the two monsters kissed. On the mouth.

'Eeew!' said Spit. 'That's disgusting!'

'Don't be so narrow-minded,' said Cherry. 'Even trolls need love. Anyway – it was you that caused it, so you can't complain.'

'This is our chance,' said Narl. 'While they're distracted.'

He led the group past the canoodling trolls, who completely ignored them, and up to the mouth of the cave. It smelled damp and stale. Water dripped from the roof and the floor was strewn with rocks and bits of wood. Beyond the entrance, the cave disappeared into a darkness thicker than treacle.

'Why can't evil-doers ever set up their base somewhere nice?' grumbled Spit. 'Or at least light.'

'Come on,' urged Alex. 'Before those arrows wear off. And don't try anything funny,' he added, giving Narl a hard look. The goblin returned a smile of butter-wouldn't-melt innocence.

One by one they scooted inside.

'Ouch!'

The gang turned. Inchy was on his hands and knees, trying to squeeze himself into the cave. He seemed to be even bigger than before. He made the trolls look like a pair of dwarfs.

'Um, Alex,' he said quietly. 'I seem to be growing faster. There's no way I can follow you into the cave. I hate confined places.'

'But we can't just leave you behind,' said Cherry.

'I don't think you've got much choice,' replied Inchy. 'Even if I could get in, what if I keep growing? I'd just get stuck and then none of us will be able to get out.'

'He's right.' Spit frowned.

'I know,' said Alex. 'But I don't like leaving him here . . .'

'I'll be fine,' said Inchy. 'I'll guard the entrance and keep an eye on the trolls. Just get back out here as quick as you can once you've got the key.'

'You sure?' said Alex.

'Sure,' Inchy said. 'Don't worry about me. I

think I'm big enough to look after myself, don't you?' He grinned weakly.

'We'll be back as soon as we can,' said Alex.

The air was cold and damp, and darkness filled every nook and cranny in the cave. The sound of dripping water echoed in the distance. Slimy mosses hung down from the ceiling, trailing against their faces as they walked. Alex led the gang on, with Narl just behind.

The floor of the cave was hard and scalloped, like a beach after the tide has gone out, making it difficult to walk on. With each step, the gang felt like they were going to topple over. To make matters worse, stones strewn everywhere tried to trip them up, and thick grey mud tugged at their feet if they strayed off the main path.

'I don't like this,' said Cherry, her voice shaking.

'I know what you mean,' said Alex. 'It's a bit spooky.'

They crept forward a little further, using their hands to feel along the walls to help guide their way.

'I can't see my hand in front of my face,' said Spit. 'How can any of this be a good idea?'

'You know,' said Alex, trying to keep the gang's mind off the horrible cave, 'some people go crawling around in caves for fun, as a hobby. It's called "spelunking".'

'That's very interesting,' said Spit, almost banging his head on a rock hanging down from the roof. 'But this isn't my idea of a fun day out.'

A sharp crack from ahead startled them all. It sounded like two stones being crashed together. Everyone stopped.

'What was that?' gasped Spit.

'It must be Shepherd,' said Narl.

'So we can't be far away, then,' said Alex.

'Look,' said House. 'There's a light down there.'

House was right. Down a tunnel on their left, a faint glow flickered from far off.

'This must be the way,' said Alex. 'Come on.'

Without hesitation, the gang turned into the new tunnel, heading for the light.

'I don't like this,' said Narl cautiously. 'It's too easy.'

'Easy?' replied Alex. 'I don't think so. Staggering around here in the pitch-dark is hardly easy. I think –'

Before Alex could reveal what he thought, Narl leapt forward and jumped on to his back, knocking him to one side. Alex fell to the ground with a thump, cracking his knees on the rocks. He tried to wriggle free, but Narl had him in a bear hug.

'House!' he gasped hoarsely. 'Help!'

House rushed forward and lifted the goblin off Alex and into the air by the scruff of his neck.

'Let me go!' hissed Narl. 'Let me explain!'

'Explain what?' spat Cherry, her voice a whisper. 'That you're working with the demon? That we're walking into a trap?'

Alex stood up and looked at the goblin.

'House, put him back on the ground, but keep hold of him.'

House did just that, making sure his grip was nice and tight.

'Well?' said Alex.

'You're right,' said Narl. 'It is a trap, but not

how you mean. Look down there on the path.'

Cautiously, Alex knelt on the cold path. For a moment, he couldn't see anything. Then, in the dim light from up ahead, he spotted a thin wire stretched from wall to wall across the path, right where he had been about to walk before Narl had jumped him. The wire was attached to a huge slab of stone suspended from the ceiling above them.

'*That's* the trap,' said Narl. 'If we'd have followed you, we'd all have been squashed flat!'

'And that would've probably hurt quite a bit,' said House, releasing Narl.

Alex shook his head disbelievingly. 'You saved us.'

Narl nodded. 'Like you said, I've got sharp eyes.'

For a moment, nobody moved. Then Alex held out his hand.

'Thanks. I'm sorry we didn't trust you.'

Narl looked at Alex's hand, then shook it. 'We're all on the same side,' he said. 'That demon has something that each of us wants, and we're going to have to work together to get them.'

'Couldn't agree more, said Alex. 'Let's go. But quietly – if we can see the light, Shepherd can't be far away.' He grinned at Narl. 'You'd best lead the way, sharp-eyes!'

With a toothy smile, Narl stepped carefully over the tripwire.

For another minute or so, the group pressed forward. The tunnel was getting lighter all the time, yellow light flickering up the walls like lizard tongues. Now they could hear a pair of voices – one meek and gentle, the other hard and flinty.

'The quiet one is Varena,' said Narl. 'I recognize her voice.'

'Then I think we can assume that the other one is the demon previously known as Mrs Shepherd,' muttered Spit.

'Can you hear what she's saying?' asked Cherry.

'Not yet,' replied Narl. 'We need to get closer.'

'OK, we're going to take this nice and quiet,' said Alex, looking at the rest of the gang. 'Try not to fall over anything, House.'

House's shoulders slumped. He looked nervous already. Alex rested a hand on the big angel's shoulder. 'But if it all kicks off, mate, we'll follow your lead, OK?'

House gave a tense smile.

'Right, follow me,' said Alex, and the gang crawled slowly forward. After about ten metres, the tunnel turned sharply to the left. Finally, it opened out into a large cavern lit with strange flaming torches that burned red, yellow and orange. The walls looked alive, blazing with colour. High above, stalactites plunged down like stone daggers stabbing through the roof. Taking cover behind a large boulder, the gang surveyed the scene.

In the centre of the cave was a strange arch, at least three metres high. It looked as if it was made from the bones of some huge creature, held together with vines and a sort of black gluey substance. There was no mistaking the fact that it was some sort of doorway. For the moment it stood silent and ominous, but the gang could almost feel the dark power radiating from it. At the very top of the arch, where the two sides met, sat a stone. And at the centre of the stone was a carved niche in the shape of a key.

Standing in front of the arch, was the demon, Mrs Shepherd.

In the gloomy cavern, she seemed even bigger than she had done in the tent of the Goblin King. Her skin seemed to glow red, like embers, and her pointed talons gleamed wickedly.

'This is not good,' moaned House softly. 'How can we fight *that*? We don't even have any silver.'

'We're not here to fight her, remember,' Alex whispered back. 'We just need to get the key back and stop her opening that portal.'

'Oh, is that all?' said Spit. 'Well, that won't be any trouble at all now, will it?'

'Goblin!' snarled Shepherd suddenly, her voice echoing like thunder. 'Bring me the key.'

From a dark corner of the cavern emerged a small goblin with long spiky hair that seemed to shoot out of her head in all directions, like an explosion. She was carrying the Key of Aziel.

'That's Varena!' whispered Narl anxiously. 'Shepherd must be forcing the princess to work for her!'

'Don't worry,' Alex reassured him. 'We'll get her out of here safely, you'll see.'

Snatching the key from Varena, Shepherd lifted it high and carefully slotted it into place at the top of the arch. Immediately, the key began to shine with a soft golden light. Fingers of energy began to reach down the sides of the arch. From the doorway in the centre came a thin wisp of mist or smoke.

'Excellent!' chuckled Shepherd. 'Soon the portal will be opened.' She turned back to Varena. 'Bring me the creature.'

'I don't like the sound of this,' whimpered House, as Varena scampered over to her dark corner and returned carrying a small metal cage. Something dark fluttered inside it.

'Is that a *bat*?' hissed Cherry incredulously.

'Yes,' said Alex, staring. 'But why does Shepherd need it?'

'I don't think you want to know,' said Spit.

As he spoke, Varena stumbled on the uneven floor of the cave. The cage dropped from her hands, and slammed into the ground. The door burst open and, with a high-pitched squeak, the bat flew out, zipped over the heads of the gang and disappeared into the darkness of the tunnels.

'Idiot!' cried Shepherd. Lashing out with her hand, she caught Varena with such a slap that the little goblin was knocked to the floor halfway across the cavern. Shepherd stood over her grimly. 'Make one more mistake,' she growled, 'and it will be *your* blood that I use to open the portal! You had better hope that I can find another, you worm!'

With that, Shepherd turned on her heel and stormed into a dark passage on the far side of the cavern.

'This is our chance,' said Alex urgently, watching as Shepherd disappeared from view. 'Let's go, Narl.'

Narl nodded, and the two of them scooted out from behind the cover of their boulder and over to Varena.

'My princess,' said Narl, as they arrived at her side. Varena looked up at Narl, obviously surprised to see him. Alex could see that she was far prettier than most of the other goblins he had met, but one side of her face was bruised and puffy where Shepherd had hit her.

'Narl?' she said. 'Why are you here? What's going on?'

'We have come to rescue you, Your Highness,' said Narl quickly. 'And to recover the key from the demon.'

Varena smiled. 'Oh, thank you,' she said. 'Thank you so much!'

Then she turned, opened her mouth and screamed, 'Mistress! Intruders!'

13
Shepherd's Spy

A thunderous roar echoed down the tunnel that Shepherd had taken.

'Quick!' yelled Spit. 'Take cover! She's coming!'

Grabbing Varena between them, Alex and Narl dived back behind the boulder where the rest of the gang were hiding.

Narl turned to Varena, his green face a mask of shock.

'What have you done, princess?'

Varena sneered. 'I've put myself at the top of

the list,' she said. 'The demon will rule the Earth, and I will rule the goblins. We've made a deal.'

'A deal with a demon?' exclaimed Cherry, stunned. 'Do you have a brain inside that crazy hairdo? You can't trust demons!'

'And what about your father, the king?' said Narl. 'He's been so worried about you.'

'That pathetic, saggy gasbag?' spat Varena. 'Pah! He's always been weak. The throne should be mine! When I am queen, the goblins will be great again! Great, I tell you!'

Spit made a sign with his finger at his head. 'I think the princess is cuckoo.'

'And who are you?' snapped Varena, rounding on Spit. 'And what's with those silly wings on that fat one, there?'

'Fat? I'm not fat,' said House. 'I'm well-built. And if you don't watch it, I'll –'

With a demonic howl, Shepherd charged back into the cavern.

'Whoever you are, you will not stop me now! Not when I am so close! The portal will open!'

With that, Shepherd casually flicked a fingertip

with a razor-sharp nail. Black demon blood spurted out on to the bones that made up the portal.

Immediately, the golden glow from the Key of Aziel brightened. The light started to trickle down the sides of the arch like honey. When it reached the floor, a burst of dazzling brightness filled the whole cavern. The gang covered their eyes. It was as if a huge firework had exploded just in front of them.

Peering out from behind the boulder, Alex could only watch as Shepherd walked over to the portal. For a moment she gazed into it, her wings billowing out behind her on waves of unseen heat. Then she threw back her head and let out an impossible cry. It was like a thousand trumpets and a thousand cannons all sounding at once. The walls of the cave shook, and a shower of pebbles and dust fell from the ceiling.

'What's she doing?' asked House, confused.

'She's calling to the demons,' murmured Spit.

For a moment, silence filled the cavern. Then, echoing from the depths of the portal, muffled as if from a great distance away, came a terrifying demonic cheer. A thousand voices raised in triumph.

'The portal is open,' said Alex disbelievingly.

'And something is coming,' added Spit, his voice shaking.

'What have you done, Varena?' cried Narl, shaking the goblin princess. 'You've destroyed us all.'

But Varena only laughed. 'Now my rule begins! And you can't stop it!'

Varena's words jolted Alex back into action.

'We'll see about that!' He turned to the others. 'Cherry, Spit – go and get help, quick! From the goblins, or Tabbris, or anyone. House and I will cause a distraction.'

Cherry started to say something but Spit grabbed her hand and yanked her away. The next second, the two were racing down the tunnel back towards open air.

'And what about me?' asked Narl.

'You should get out too. Take Varena and go.'

'No way!' snapped Narl. 'We're all in this together, remember?'

Varena laughed. 'And you'll all suffer together! All of you! Fools!'

Narl pulled a ragged handkerchief from his coat pocket and stuffed it into Varena's mouth. 'I think that's enough chat from you, princess,' he said.

The outraged expression on Varena's face was so comical that even under the dangerous circumstances, Alex couldn't help but laugh. But at exactly the same moment, the boulder they were hiding behind exploded.

'Where are you hiding, you rats!' boomed Shepherd's voice.

Alex felt himself fly through the air, spinning and turning. He landed with a painful thump on the hard stone floor of the cavern, just in front of the portal. Alex tried to focus his eyes, but his vision was swimming. He couldn't see anyone – House, Narl and Varena weren't there any more.

Then, painfully, he managed to get up on to all fours, and found himself staring directly into the portal. It was a terrifying sight. The portal was at one end of an enormous passage made entirely of roaring flames. The passage stretched down, down, down into darkness. And marching up the passageway, were ranks and ranks of demons. They were still so far away that they were tiny, but the sound of their feet was like the rumble of distant thunder and they moved forward like a swarm of army ants. And they were heading straight for the portal – straight for Earth.

Alex edged away, trying desperately to collect his thoughts. If he could just come up with a plan . . . But his mind was blank, and before he could even begin to think, the demonic shape of Mrs Shepherd stepped forward to face him, crushing rocks to dust beneath her feet.

'So, boy. You are the one who has dared to come here?' Shepherd laughed horribly. 'What foolishness!'

With the sound of creaking leather, Shepherd slowly crouched down to look at Alex more closely. Alex stared up into her face. It was twisted with hate, the eyes burning like coals. He was literally rooted to the spot with terror. There was no escape.

Then a loud voice boomed through the cave: 'Stand away from the portal and put your claws in the air! This is Captain Fairfax of Angelic Special Operations – you are surrounded!'

14
Showdown

The demon whipped round.

'Impossible! Where are you? Show yourself!'

Alex gasped for breath, relief flooding through him. Spit and Cherry must have somehow got word back to Tabbris already. Special Ops had arrived! Reinforcements from Heaven! Shepherd would soon be wishing she'd never been spawned. Once the demon was dealt with, the portal would be closed and the Earth would be saved. Maybe, thought Alex, they might even agree to take the gang home to Heaven – after all, it was thanks to them that Shepherd's evil plot had been discovered.

Rubbing his neck, Alex turned to look for his rescuers. It was still dark in the cavern, and at first he couldn't spot them. Then he saw the massive figure standing in the shadows at the entrance to the tunnel the gang had used to come in. Captain Fairfax was tall and broad-shouldered, and Alex could see the outline of his vast, feathered wings fluttering in the hot wind blowing from the portal.

'You'll never win,' boomed Fairfax defiantly. 'Spec Ops are here, and you're really stuffed. How does it feel to be such a total loser?'

'Big talk,' said Shepherd, circling around the cavern towards Fairfax. 'But good can't win every time! One day you will fail. And then . . .' She laughed, a wisp of smoke billowing from her mouth.

Alex backed away to the edge of the cave. It didn't look as if Shepherd was going to give up without a fight, and he didn't want to get in the way.

But Fairfax wasn't coming forward to attack. In fact, he was circling around the cavern in the *opposite* direction to Shepherd, keeping to the shadows. Alex frowned. What was happening?

'Give it up, demon!' barked Fairfax. 'I want that key.'

Shepherd's eyes darkened. She reached out a blackened and leathery hand and cracked her knuckles.

'Come and take it, then!'

Cherry bolted from the cave, with Spit at her heels.

'Where's Inchy?'

'I can't see him,' gasped Spit. 'And it's not like he should be difficult to spot, is it?'

'Neither can I,' said Cherry, straining her eyes into the trees around them. 'What do we do? Alex needs help NOW!' She kicked at a fallen tree trunk in frustration.

'Ow!'

'Woah!' said Spit, startled. 'That tree you just kicked – it spoke!'

'Don't be idiotic,' said Cherry. 'Trees don't . . .'

Her voice died away as, with the splintering sound of several falling trees, Inchy raised himself up off the ground where he had been lying and stood up.

Spit looked at Cherry.

'No way.'

'Way.'

What Cherry had mistaken for a fallen tree was actually one of Inchy's legs. And now he was standing, he towered above them, impossibly high. He was taller than the surrounding trees and didn't look very pleased about it in the slightest.

'You're, er, still growing, then?' said Spit. It was something of an understatement. Inchy had to be twenty-five or thirty metres tall.

'I know,' said Inchy. 'And I can't move around or anything. I'm too big and too strong. Whatever I touch just breaks. It's a nightmare.'

'Well, *now* what are we going to do?' asked Cherry. 'Alex sent us to find help, not someone the size of a small mountain!'

Spit's eyes lit up.

'What?' said Cherry.

'I have a plan.'

'Don't start that!' yelled Cherry. 'You're not Alex.'

'No, I'm not,' said Spit. 'Which is why this plan will work.'

Back in the cave, Shepherd and Captain Fairfax were still circling each other warily. Like two lions about to battle it out.

The demon chuckled. 'You pure lights are all the same, aren't you? Always so goody-goody and so sure that you're doing the right thing. Don't you ever get bored?'

'Er . . . Not really, no,' said Fairfax.

Alex felt a shiver of doubt race through him. He'd read about Special Operations angels ever since he'd joined Cloud Nine Academy. They were the best of the best – the fiercest demon butt-kickers in the business. He'd always expected them to be a bit more, well, confident. If he wasn't mistaken, Fairfax sounded nervous.

'Don't you ever wish that you could break a

few rules now and again?' continued Shepherd, her voice soft and tempting. 'Just to find out what it's like?'

'Um . . . no thanks,' came the reply.

Alex was now more than a little afraid. Something was wrong. Maybe Fairfax was on his own – an advance guard. Perhaps he was waiting for backup before trying to tackle Shepherd. But somehow Alex didn't think that was it. And why was he staying in the shadows?

Alex swallowed hard. The darkness of the cavern felt like it was trying to suffocate him. He eyed the portal nervously. While Shepherd was keeping Fairfax talking, the demons inside were getting closer and closer. He could hear their voices now, harsh and cruel, calling to each other as they raced towards the doorway that would lead them on to Earth. A hot wind swept outwards from it, making the torches lighting the cave flicker.

Shepherd prowled forward, like a huge tiger tracking its prey. 'Come on, angel,' she hissed. 'Why are you hiding in the shadows? Do you like the darkness? It's warm and soft, isn't it? It cloaks you and hides you. You can get away with anything in the dark . . . Anything! Perhaps you would like to join me?'

'That's enough!' said Fairfax. 'Give up now, or else!'

'Or else what?' snarled Shepherd. 'I'm too close! Far too close to let an irritating do-gooder like you ruin my plans!'

With that, Shepherd sprang, letting out an ear-splitting shriek. Her wings buffeted the torches, sending a cloud of sparks into the air. Smoke billowed in a choking cloud, and Captain Fairfax stepped out of the shadows.

Alex gasped. There was no mistaking the features of the angelic hero who had arrived in the nick of time to save the day.

Captain Fairfax was House.

Alex's heart jumped into his mouth. No wonder his friend had been trying to stay in the darkness – he was big enough to be mistaken for a full angel so long as Shepherd couldn't see his face. The daft idiot was taking on the demon single-handed.

'I see you now!' raged the demon, flames pouring from her throat. Alex screamed as Shepherd leapt towards House like a burning arrow, talons outstretched.

'Whoa!' cried House, diving out of the way as Shepherd's claws struck the wall, sending sparks flying. Rolling across the floor of the cave in a tangle of arms and legs, he barely had time to stumble to his feet before Shepherd launched herself at him a second time. House tried to sidestep, but Shepherd was too fast. She was on him in a flash, pinning him to the ground with one of her clawed feet. House struggled against the weight of the demon, but it was no use. He was trapped. The demon bent down, lowering her face until it was only centimetres away from his. For a moment she froze, as if she couldn't believe what she was seeing. Then she staggered backwards in shock.

'But . . . You're just a boy!' she howled.

Released, House jumped upright. Setting his feet, he stood between Shepherd and the portal, attempting the fiercest face he could do.

'I'm not a boy!' he cried. 'I'm a Guardian Angel!'

Behind him, his wings burst into view, blazing white in the gloom and silhouetted against the fiery light spewing from the portal.

'Pah! A set of wings doesn't make you an angel, child!' spat Shepherd. 'As you will learn . . .'

Alex glanced at the portal. The sound of demons, like a stampede of pigs racing towards the arch, was getting louder and louder every second. Alex could see shapes approaching the doorway now – black shadows laced with fire.

Shepherd lunged at House. He ducked, then swung his wings round, sending her tumbling into the cave wall.

The demon roared.

'This is your last warning,' puffed House, looking rather red in the face. 'I'm a black belt in origami. Surrender now before I have to get really tough.'

Alex cringed. House had probably meant to say 'karate'. Alex would have to explain the difference between martial arts and paper models later – if they got out of this alive. Shepherd just looked momentarily confused.

'Surrender?' shrieked the demon, ignoring House's not–very–scary threat. 'To a child? Never!'

Again Shepherd came at him, slashing with her claws. Again, House was quick enough to dodge, this time following it up with a punch to the jaw that sent her to her knees with a howl.

Alex was amazed – his best friend was kicking a Fire Demon in the pants! He caught House's eye and gave him a thumbs up. With a quick grin, House returned the gesture. And tripped.

'No!' groaned Alex, but it was too late. House tumbled backwards, landing hard on his back in a pile of rubble. Shepherd spread her bat–like wings and flew into the air, sweeping down to stand astride him.

'Whose turn is it to surrender now, little angel?' sneered Shepherd, and swung her hand down in a deadly arc.

The roof of the cave exploded.

Alex dived for cover as huge chunks of stone fell through the air like confetti. Coughing and spluttering, he looked up to see what had caused it.

An enormous hand, the size of a small car, had burst through the ceiling from outside. As Alex watched, it seized Shepherd in a vice-like grip, dragging her away from House. Shepherd screamed and thrashed, but she was unable to break free.

'It's Inchy!' yelled Alex, catching a glimpse of a huge face with tufty hair and freckles through the hole in the roof. 'It's Inchy's hand! He's got her!'

'Quick, Alex!' cried House. 'Get the key! Close the portal!'

Alex made for the glowing arch. On the other side of the portal, the demons were close enough for Alex to see their red eyes glowing as they raced towards the world. Flames licked around the sides of the doorway, threatening to break through. There was no time to feel fear. No time to think at all. Clambering up one side of the arch, he reached for the key.

'No!' screamed a voice. 'It's mine! Mine!'

From the far corner of the cavern, Varena ran

forward, with Narl in hot pursuit. Grabbing Alex's leg, she pulled him back down to the ground with a thump. 'You can't have it,' she shrieked. 'It's mine and I'll use it to rule the world!'

Pushing Alex aside, Varena scrambled up the side of the arch herself, her fingers groping hungrily towards the Key of Aziel.

'Not so fast, Your Highness!' cried Narl, seizing Varena from behind. 'We have to get out of here!'

A loud cry of pain echoed around the cave. Everyone turned to look. Inchy was still holding tightly to Mrs Shepherd, but now her whole body seemed to be on fire – a last desperate attempt to break free.

'I can't hold her!' shouted Inchy. 'She's burning me!'

With a flick of his wrist, Inchy threw the flaming demon away from him, as far across the cavern as he could. She soared over the heads of Alex and House, slammed hard on to the floor – and bounced into the portal. As she fell, her wings clipped the sides of the arch, causing it to collapse behind her. With a scream,

Varena and Narl tumbled into the disintegrating portal.

There was a blinding flash that was so bright it almost felt like daylight. As it faded, Alex and House pulled themselves to their feet, rubbing their eyes.

Nothing was left of the portal except a pile of scorched, broken bones. Shepherd, Varena and Narl were gone.

15
The Final Wish

Alex staggered to his feet and went over to help House up.

'I can't believe what you just did. That's the bravest thing I've ever seen,' he said. 'And the stupidest. What were you thinking?'

'I *wasn't* thinking,' admitted House. 'I was just doing. You said we had to cause a distraction to keep the demon busy while Spit and Cherry got help. And then I remembered that I had my wings back, and that they could be useful, even if I can't fly. I reckoned I might be able to fool the demon for a few minutes, and it worked.'

Alex threw a tight hug round House, who returned it enthusiastically for a moment. Then he gave an embarrassed cough and let go.

'That's enough hugging, I think,' he mumbled.

'Erm, yeah,' said Alex, looking equally embarrassed. 'Anyway, well done, mate. I thought you were going to be squashed into angel paste!'

'So did I,' said House solemnly. Then he grinned. 'Exciting, wasn't it?'

'Look,' said Alex, walking across the cavern to the collapsed arch. 'It's the key.'

It was true. The Key of Aziel lay on the ground, glinting faintly in the torchlight.

'Must've been thrown clear when the portal was destroyed.'

House joined Alex as he picked it up.

'Looks so small and normal, doesn't it?' he said. 'Hard to believe it just opened a door to the Other Side.'

'What about Narl and Varena?' said House

quietly. 'Do you think they're down there too . . . ?'

'I don't know.' Alex bit his lip. 'They all tumbled together into the portal just before it collapsed.'

'It's so unfair. Narl helped us – he saved us from that tripwire trap.'

Alex shook his head sadly. 'I know.' He looked at the tunnel that led out of the cavern. 'I reckon we should go and find the others now though.'

'OK.' House nodded.

'Do you think it's morning yet?' asked Alex as he led the way.

'I don't care what time of day it is,' replied House. 'All I know is that my body is positively demanding a full English breakfast.'

'How can you think of food at a time like this?'

'It takes practice.' House smiled.

Outside the cave it was still dark, the moon offering the only light. Inchy was sitting on the ground in a small clearing near the cave entrance, sucking his burned hand. Spit stood some distance away, eyeing his colossal friend nervously. Alex could understand why – even sitting down, Inchy's head poked out above the tree tops. Cherry was nowhere to be seen.

'Well,' said Alex, brushing his hands together, 'that's another demon thwarted!'

'Thanks to my brains and Inchy's brawn,' Spit shot back. 'Where are Varena and Narl?'

Alex shook his head. 'They didn't make it. They fell into the portal just before it closed.'

'We've got the key, though,' said House. 'So why is Inchy still huge? And why is Spit still in Cherry's body?'

'Just having the key back doesn't help us,' Alex pointed out. 'We need to find out how to undo the chaos magic.'

'I think we might be able to help with that,' said Cherry, striding into the clearing. Serena was at her side.

'Oh my word!' screamed the white witch when she saw Inchy. 'It's a giant! We're all going to die!'

Cherry grabbed her before she could run away.

'It's not a giant, it's Inchy,' she explained. 'Remember? You met him earlier tonight, except then he was about fifty times smaller than he is now.'

'Oh, yes, sorry,' said Serena. 'Sorry. This whole experience has made me a little bit jumpy.'

Cherry looked at Alex, whose clothes were muddy and singed from the fight in the cave.

'What happened? Are you OK?'

'I'm fine,' said Alex. 'It's House and Inchy who are the real heroes. But we'll talk about all that later.' He turned to Serena. 'Did you find anything about how to undo the wishes?'

'I did . . .' replied Serena slowly. 'But I don't think you're going to like it.'

'Why not?'

Serena sighed. 'I found another old book about mythical objects and it had few pages on the Key of Aziel. Apparently, the chaos that it creates is irreversible. The only way to undo it is to destroy the key.'

'Is that all? We just defeated a Fire Demon and

saved the world from a horde of demons,' laughed House. 'I think we can handle a key.'

Serena shook her head. 'But the book said that the key was almost impossible to destroy.'

'How come?' asked Spit.

Serena produced a small, leather-bound book from a pouch hanging from her waist. She leafed through it until she found the right page.

'It says here that the Key of Aziel was forged by the Firbolgs of Norway, giants with the strength of twenty men. Only one with the same strength can break it.'

'But we can't stay like this,' said Spit. 'I don't want to be a girl forever.'

'I'm not exactly thrilled about being a boy,' retorted Cherry.

'Just a minute,' said Alex. 'I think I've got an idea.'

Everyone turned.

'Are you sure this is the right time and place for one of your ideas?' asked Cherry.

'It's never the right time or place,' said Spit. 'But what choice have we got?'

'You say the key was forged by giants?' Alex asked Serena.

Serena nodded.

'And that only a giant can break it?'

She nodded again.

'Problem solved, then!' crowed Alex.

'I don't know if you've noticed,' said Cherry through gritted teeth, 'but we haven't got a giant, have we . . .' Her voice trailed away as she looked up at Inchy's huge face beaming down through the trees.

Alex grinned smugly. 'We don't have a *real* giant, no. But we have the next best thing.'

Alex craned his head back. 'Inchy?' he called, holding up the Key of Aziel. 'Reckon you could break this?'

'I'll give it a go.'

A huge hand reached down, like a lift descending from the tree tops. Alex placed the key between Inchy's thumb and forefinger, which were both as big as a bed.

'OK, stand back, everyone,' said Alex. 'We don't know what's going to happen.'

For a few seconds, everything was still, as if the woods themselves were holding their breath. Then Inchy pressed down on the key.

There was a faint crack, like a breaking twig, followed by a sweeping gust of wind that billowed through the trees, swirling up leaves and grass. The gang held on to each other as it tugged at their clothes and hair. Then the wind died and all was quiet.

'Easy,' said Inchy, holding his hand out.

Lying in his palm, the Key of Aziel was snapped neatly in two.

'I hate to be the one to point this out,' said Cherry, 'but nothing's changed. I'm still in Spit's body, Inchy's still huge and House has still got wings.'

'It didn't work,' moaned House. 'We're stuck like this forever. How am I supposed to go to human school with wings? Everyone will take the mickey.'

Alex couldn't believe it. What had gone wrong?

It was Inchy who worked it out.

'Hang on a minute, guys!' he cried, his huge voice echoing through the woods like a foghorn. 'We've got this wrong. Serena's book didn't say that destroying the key would undo the magic, just that it would undo the *chaos*.'

'What's the difference?' asked Spit.

'Well, the whole problem with the bracelets wasn't the wishes, it was the fact that the key was making the wishes come true in strange ways – because of the chaos.'

'So what?' huffed Cherry.

'So now the key's been destroyed, the wishes might work properly!' said Inchy excitedly.

'Maybe,' agreed Alex. 'But we were only granted one wish each and we've used them all up.'

'No we haven't,' said Spit. 'I never used mine. It was you lot who caused all the trouble, as usual.'

Cherry clapped her hands with glee. 'Then what are you waiting for? Wish us back to normal!'

Spit grinned slyly. 'What's it worth?'

Cherry's eyes bulged.

'What?!' she demanded.

'Well, it's the last wish and I've got it. Sound's

pretty valuable to me. Maybe worth everyone else doing my cleaning chores for the rest of the month?'

'I'll tell you what it's worth,' fumed Cherry. 'It's worth me not telling everyone at school on Monday that you spent Halloween wearing frilly knickers!'

Spit looked horrified. 'You wouldn't dare!'

'Try me,' said Cherry, folding her arms.

'But it's not like I *chose* to wear them!' protested Spit. 'It's not my fault that we swapped bodies.'

'I know that,' snapped Cherry. 'But I don't think you'll be able to explain it to the rest of the class, will you?'

'All right, you win,' grumbled Spit. Then his face fell. 'Seriously though, what if destroying the key has destroyed the magic as well as the chaos?'

Alex puffed out his cheeks. 'There's only one way to find out. Try it, mate.'

Spit went silent for a minute, thinking of exactly the right words to use. Then he spoke:

'I wish that everything was back the way it's supposed to be.'

For a moment, nothing happened. The gang held their breath – was it only the chaos that had been destroyed when the key was snapped, or had the wish magic died too?

With a flash, the bracelet burst into light. Everyone threw up their hands, blinded for an instant.

Alex was the first to open his eyes. It took a couple of seconds for him to focus, but soon the blurry shapes made sense and he could make out the rest of the gang. But something was missing. Something big.

'Where's Inchy?' he asked.

The clearing where Inchy had been sitting was empty.

'Over there!' cried House. 'Look!'

The clearing wasn't quite empty after all. A normal-sized Inchy was struggling to clamber over a fallen tree as he made his way towards his friends. Before he could get there, though, Spit and Cherry suddenly screamed and jumped in the air at the same time.

'I'm me!' yelled Spit. 'Look! It's me! I'm

wearing trousers again! I'm in my own body! Brilliant!'

'I've never felt so happy, ever,' said Cherry, spinning around. 'And I don't ever, *ever* want to be a boy again.'

Inchy joined them. 'And I never thought I'd say it, but it's actually quite nice being small.'

House glanced behind him. His snowy wings were gone. For a moment he felt a twinge of sadness. It had been nice to feel like a proper angel again. But having wings and not being able to fly was no fun at all. He sighed. He'd just have to wait until the gang got back to Cloud Nine and he could enjoy having wings properly.

With his head turned over his shoulder, though, House was the first person to notice two small figures emerging from the cave mouth.

His eyes popped. 'It's Narl and Varena!' he cried. 'They're back!'

The gang spun round. It was true. The two goblins looked grimy and exhausted, but they were alive. Narl had used his long brown jacket to tie Varena's hands together and was dragging her behind him.

'It's your wish,' said Alex to Spit. 'You wished for every*thing* to be back the way it was supposed to be! It must have saved Narl and Varena too.'

'But then what about Shepherd?' said House, his eyes wide with worry. 'Won't she be back as well?'

'I doubt it.' Inchy grinned. 'Think about it. Goblins are supposed to live on Earth, but where is a demon *supposed* to live? The Other Side! I think we're safe. For now.'

'Welcome back!' said Alex, as the goblins reached the gang. 'Are you OK?'

Narl shuddered. 'Let's just say, I'm glad to be home.'

Cherry looked at Varena, who was now sitting on the ground behind Narl. The goblin princess looked utterly deflated.

'What are you going to do with her, Narl?'

'Take her home,' he growled. 'It'll break her father's heart to find out that she was planning to depose him. But it's up to him to decide what to do with her now.'

At that moment, a familiar voice echoed through the woods.

'I know you're here somewhere!' it bellowed. 'How dare you go AWOL on my watch! I'll have you on triple gardening chores for a month!'

'Oh, good,' said Cherry. 'It's Tabbris.'

Alex sighed and turned to Serena, Narl and Verena. 'He's our guardian, and we're in big, big trouble. It's probably best if you three disappear.'

'Goodbye to you all,' said Serena. 'It's been a Halloween that I'll never forget. Do drop in at the shop and see me sometime.' With a wave, the white witch slipped away through the trees, heading back towards Green Hill.

'Well, Narl,' said Spit, shaking the goblin by the hand. 'Thanks for all your help – and for not eating us.'

Narl grinned. 'Oh, that,' he laughed. 'I was just joking – don't you know that all goblins are vegetarian?'

'What?!'

Cherry and Inchy burst out laughing at the shocked expression on Spit's face.

'See you around, guys!' said Narl. 'Next time the Goblin Market is in town, the veggie pies are on me!'

'I'll remember that.' House smiled.

Tugging Varena after him, Narl disappeared into the darkness in the direction of the Midnight Fair.

'Attention! Attention! Alex, Cherry, Big House, Inchy and Respite – hand yourselves in immediately! This is not a drill! Repeat – this is not a drill!'

It sounded as if Tabbris was now using a megaphone. The beam of a torch stabbed between the trees, trying to pin the gang down.

'Do you reckon he'll ever realize that when we get into trouble it's only because we're saving the world?' asked Alex.

'Oh, so *that's* what we were doing,' said Spit. 'I had wondered.'

'Come on,' said Alex. 'Time to face the music. Let's go.'

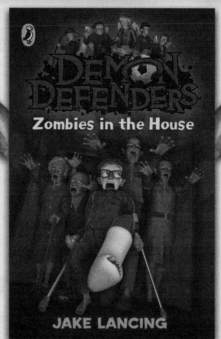

It all started with a Scarecrow

Puffin is well over sixty years old.
Sounds ancient, doesn't it? But Puffin has never been
so lively. We're always on the lookout for the next big
idea, which is how it began all those years ago.

Penguin Books was a big idea from the mind of
a man called Allen Lane, who in 1935 invented
the quality paperback and changed the world.
**And from great Penguins, great Puffins grew,
changing the face of children's books forever.**

The first four Puffin Picture Books were hatched in 1940 and the
first Puffin story book featured a man with broomstick arms called
Worzel Gummidge. In 1967 Kaye Webb, Puffin Editor, started the
Puffin Club, promising to **'make children into readers'**.
She kept that promise and over 200,000 children became
devoted Puffineers through their quarterly installments of
Puffin Post, which is now back for a new generation.

Many years from now, we hope you'll look back and
remember Puffin with a smile. **No matter what your age
or what you're into, there's a Puffin for everyone.**
The possibilities are endless, but one thing is for sure:
whether it's a picture book or a paperback, a sticker book
or a hardback, **if it's got that little Puffin
on it – it's bound to be good.**